THE NOTEBOOK

D1423630

Agota Kristof, born in Csikvánd, Hungary, in 1935, became an exile in French-speaking Switzerland in 1956. Working in a factory, she slowly learned the language of her adopted country. Her first novel, *The Notebook* (1986), gained international recognition and was translated into more than thirty languages. Later work included plays and stories as well as *The Proof* and *The Third Lie* (published by CBe as *2 Novels*), which complete the trilogy begun with *The Notebook*. She died in 2011.

Kristof's *The Illiterate*, her memoir of how she came to write *The Notebook*, is also available from CBe.

Alan Sheridan has translated over fifty books, including works by Sartre, Lacan, Foucault and Robbe-Grillet. In 2004 he was awarded the Prix du rayonnement de la langue française by the Académie Française, for services to the French language and its literature.

Slavoj Žižek is a Slovene cultural critic and philosopher who has written widely on politics and cultural studies.

also by Agota Kristof

FICTION
The Proof
The Third Lie
Yesterday

MEMOIR
The Illiterate

Agota Kristof

The Notebook

translated from the French by Alan Sheridan

afterword by Slavoj Žižek

ⒷB *editions*

This edition published in Great Britain in 2014
by CB editions
146 Percy Road London W12 9QL
www.cbeditions.com

Originally published in French as *Le Grand Cahier*
in 1986 by Editions du Seuil
This translation originally published by Methuen London

Printed in England by Imprint Digital, Exeter EX5 5HY

ISBN 978-0-9573266-9-9

The Notebook   1

SLAVOJ ŽIŽEK Afterword   163

The Notebook

Arrival at Grandmother's

We arrive from the Big Town. We've been travelling all night. Mother's eyes are red. She's carrying a big cardboard box and we two boys are each carrying a small suitcase containing our clothes, plus Father's big dictionary, which we take it in turns to carry since our arms get tired.

We walk for a long time. Grandmother's house is a long way from the station, at the other end of the Little Town. There are no trams, buses or cars here. Just a few army trucks driving around.

There aren't many people in the streets. The town is very quiet. Our footsteps echo on the pavement; we walk, without speaking, Mother in the middle, between the two of us.

When we get to Grandmother's garden gate, Mother says:

'Wait for me here.'

We wait for a while, then we go into the garden, walk round the house, and crouch down under a window, where we can hear voices. We hear Mother say:

'There's nothing more to eat at home, no bread, no meat, no vegetables, no milk. Nothing. I can't feed them any more.'

Another voice says:

'So you've remembered me. For ten years you didn't give me a thought. You never came. You never wrote.'

Mother says:

'You know why. I *loved* Father.'

The other voice says:

'Yes, and now you remember that you also have a mother. You come here and ask me to help you.'

Mother says:

'I'm not asking anything for myself. I just want my children to survive this war. The Big Town is being bombed night and day, and there's no food left. All the children are being evacuated to the country, with relations or with strangers, anywhere.'

The other voice says:

'So why didn't you send them to strangers, anywhere?'

Mother says:

'They're your grandsons.'

'My grandsons? I don't even know them. How many are there?'

'Two. Two boys. Twins.'

The other voice asks:

'What have you done with the others?'

Mother asks:

'What others?'

'Bitches have four or five puppies at a time. You keep one or two and drown the others.'

The other voice laughs loudly. Mother says nothing, then the other voice asks:

'They have a father, at least? You aren't married, as far as I know. I wasn't invited to any wedding.'

'I am married. Their father is at the front. I haven't had any news of him for six months.'

'Then you can put a cross over him.'

The other voice laughs again. Mother starts crying. We go back to the garden gate.

Mother comes out of the house with an old woman.

Mother says to us:

4

'This is your grandmother. You'll be staying with her for a while – till the end of the war.'

Grandmother says:

'It could last a long time. But I'll put them to work, don't you fret. Food isn't free here either.'

Mother says:

'I'll send you money. Their clothes are in the suitcases. And there are sheets and blankets in the box. Be good, you two. I'll write to you.'

She kisses us and goes away, crying.

Grandmother laughs very loudly and says:

'Sheets and blankets! White shirts and patent-leather shoes! I'll teach you what life is about!'

We stick out our tongues at Grandmother. She laughs even louder and slaps her thighs.

Grandmother's House

Grandmother's house is five minutes' walk from the last houses in the Little Town. After that, there is nothing but the dusty road, blocked a bit further on by a barrier. It is forbidden to go any further, a soldier is on guard there. He has a machine-gun and binoculars and, when it rains, he takes shelter in a sentry box. We know that beyond the barrier, hidden by the trees, there's a secret military base and, beyond the base, the frontier of another country.

Grandmother's house is surrounded by a garden, at the bottom of which there is a stream, then the forest.

The garden contains all sorts of vegetables and fruit trees. In a corner, there's a hutch, a hen-house, a pigsty and a hut for the goats. We have tried to climb on to the back of one of the biggest pigs, but it's impossible to stay on.

The vegetables, the fruit, the rabbits, the ducks and the chickens are sold at the market by Grandmother, as well as the hens' and ducks' eggs and the goat's cheese. The pigs are sold to the butcher, who pays for them with money, or with hams and smoked sausage.

There is also a dog to keep away thieves and a cat to keep away mice and rats. We mustn't give the cat anything to eat, so that he's always hungry.

Grandmother also owns a vineyard on the other side of the road.

You enter the house through the kitchen, which is large and warm. A fire burns all day long in the wood-stove. Near the window there's a huge table and a corner bench.

We sleep on the bench.

From the kitchen a door leads to Grandmother's bedroom, but it's always locked. Only Grandmother goes into it and, even then, only at night, to sleep.

There's another room, which can be reached without going through the kitchen, directly from the garden. This room is occupied by a foreign officer. The door to that room is also locked.

Under the house there's a cellar full of things to eat and, under the roof, an attic where Grandmother doesn't go any more since we sawed away one of the rungs of the ladder and she fell and hurt herself. The entrance to the attic is just above the officer's door and we get up there by means of a rope. It's there that we hide the notebook, Father's dictionary and the other things we have to hide.

We have now made a key, which opens all the doors in the house, and made holes in the attic floor. With the key we can move freely about the house when nobody's in and, through the holes, we can observe Grandmother and the officer in their rooms, without anybody knowing.

Grandmother

Grandmother is Mother's mother. Before coming to live in her house, we didn't even know that Mother still had a mother.

We call her Grandmother.

People call her the Witch. She calls us 'sons of a bitch'.

Grandmother is small and thin. She has a black shawl on her head. Her clothes are dark grey. She wears old army shoes. When it's fine, she walks barefoot. Her face is covered with wrinkles, brown spots and warts with hairs growing out of them. She has no teeth left, at least none that can be seen.

Grandmother never washes. She wipes her mouth with the corner of her shawl when she has finished eating or drinking. She doesn't wear knickers. When she wants to urinate, she just stops wherever she happens to be, spreads her legs and pisses on the ground under her skirt. Of course, she doesn't do it in the house.

Grandmother never undresses. We have watched her in her room at night. She takes off one skirt and there's another skirt underneath. She takes off her blouse and there's another one underneath. She goes to bed like that. She doesn't take off her shawl.

Grandmother doesn't say much. Except in the evening. In the evening, she takes a bottle down from a shelf and drinks straight out of it. Soon she starts to talk in a language we don't know. It's not the language that the foreign soldiers speak, it's a quite different language.

In that unknown language, Grandmother asks herself questions and answers them. Sometimes she laughs, sometimes she gets angry and starts shouting. In the end, almost always, she starts crying, she staggers into her room, drops on to her bed and we hear her sobbing long into the night.

Our Tasks

We have to do certain jobs for Grandmother, otherwise she doesn't give us anything to eat and leaves us to spend the night out of doors.

But at first we refuse to obey her. We sleep in the garden, and eat fruit and raw vegetables.

In the morning, before daybreak, we see Grandmother leave the house. She says nothing to us. She goes and feeds the animals, milks the goats, then takes them to the edge of the stream, where she ties them to a tree. Then she waters the garden and picks the vegetables and fruit, which she loads into her wheelbarrow. She also puts on to it a basket full of eggs, a small cage with a rabbit, and a chicken or duck with its legs tied together.

She goes off to the market, pushing her wheelbarrow with the strap around her scrawny neck, which forces her head down. She staggers under the weight. The bumps and stones in the road make her lose her balance, but she goes on walking, her feet turned inwards, like a duck. She walks to the town, to the market, without stopping, without putting her wheelbarrow down once.

When she gets back from the market, she makes a soup with the vegetables she hasn't sold and jams with the fruit. She eats, she goes and has a nap in her vineyard, she sleeps for an hour, then she works in the vineyard or, if there is nothing to do there, she comes back to the house, she cuts wood, she feeds the animals again, she brings back the goats, she milks them, she goes out into the forest, comes back with mushrooms and kindling, she makes cheeses, she dries mushrooms and beans, she bottles other vegetables, waters the garden again, puts things away in the cellar and so on until nightfall.

On the sixth morning, when she leaves the house, we have already watered the garden. We take heavy buckets full of pig-feed from her, we take the goats to the edge of the stream, we help her load the wheelbarrow. When she comes back from the market, we are cutting wood.

At the meal, Grandmother says:

'Now you know you have to earn your board and lodging.'

We say:

'It's not that. The work is hard, but to watch someone working and not do anything is even harder, especially if it's someone old.'

Grandmother sniggers:

'Sons of a bitch! You mean you felt sorry for me?'

'No, Grandmother. We just felt ashamed.'

In the afternoon we go and gather wood in the forest.

From now on we do all the work we can.

The Forest and the Stream

The forest is very big, the stream is very small. To get to the forest, we have to cross the stream. When there isn't much water, we can cross it by jumping from one stone to another but, sometimes, when it has rained a lot, the water reaches up to our waist, and this water is cold and muddy. We decide to build a bridge with bricks and planks that we find around bombed houses.

Our bridge is strong. We show it to Grandmother. She tests it and says:

'Very good. But don't go too far into the forest. The frontier is nearby and the soldiers will shoot at you. And above all, don't get lost. I won't come looking for you.'

When we were building the bridge, we saw fish. They hide under big stones or in the shadow of bushes and trees, whose branches meet in places over the stream. We choose the biggest fish. We catch them and put them in a watering-can filled with water. In the evening, when we take them back to the house, Grandmother says:

'Sons of a bitch! How did you catch them?'

'With our hands; it's easy. You just have to stay still and wait.'

'Then catch a lot. As many as you can.'

Next day, Grandmother puts the watering-can on her wheelbarrow and she sells our fish at the market.

We often go into the forest, we never get lost, we know where the frontier is. Soon the guards get to know us. They never shoot at us. Grandmother teaches us to know the difference between mushrooms you can eat and the poisonous ones.

From the forest we bring back firewood on our backs, and mushrooms and chestnuts in baskets. We stack the wood neatly against the walls of the house under the lean-to and we roast chestnuts on the stove if Grandmother isn't there.

Once, in the forest, beside a big hole made by a bomb, we find a dead soldier. He is still all of a piece, only his eyes have gone because of the crows. We take his rifle, his cartridges and his grenades: we hide the rifle inside a bundle of firewood, and the cartridges and grenades in our baskets, under the mushrooms.

When we get back to Grandmother's, we carefully wrap these objects in straw and potato sacks, and bury them under the seat, in front of the officer's window.

Dirt

At home, in the Big Town, Mother often used to wash us. In the shower or in the bath. She put clean clothes on us and cut our nails. She used to go with us to the barber's to have our hair cut. We used to brush our teeth after every meal.

At Grandmother's it is impossible to wash. There is no bathroom, there isn't even any running water. We have to go and pump water from the well in the yard, and carry it back in a bucket. There is no soap in the house, no toothpaste, no washing powder.

Everything in the kitchen is dirty. The red, irregular tiles stick to our feet, the big table sticks to our hands and elbows. The stove is completely black with grease and the walls all around are black with soot. Although Grandmother washes the dishes, the plates, spoons and knives are never quite clean and the saucepans are covered with a thick layer of grime. The dishcloths are discoloured and have a nasty smell.

At first we didn't even want to eat, especially when we saw how Grandmother cooked the meals, wiping her nose on her sleeve and never washing her hands. Now we take no notice.

When it's warm we go and bathe in the stream, we wash our faces and clean our teeth in the well. When it's cold, it's impossible to wash properly. There is no receptacle big enough in the house. Our sheets, our blankets and our towels have disappeared. We never see again the big cardboard box in which Mother brought them.

Grandmother has sold everything.

We're getting dirtier and dirtier, our clothes too. We take clean clothes out of our suitcases under the seat, but soon there are no clean clothes left. Those we are wearing are getting torn and our shoes are wearing through. When possible, we walk barefoot and wear only underpants or trousers. The soles of our feet are getting hard, we no longer feel thorns or stones. Our skin is getting brown, our legs and arms are covered with scratches, cuts, scabs and insect bites. Our nails, which are never cut, break, and our hair, which is almost white because of the sun, reaches down to our shoulders.

The privy is at the bottom of the garden. There's never any paper. We wipe ourselves with the biggest leaves from certain plants.

We smell of a mixture of manure, fish, grass, mushrooms, smoke, milk, cheese, mud, clay, earth, sweat, urine and mould.

We smell bad, like Grandmother.

Exercise to Toughen the Body

Grandmother often hits us, with her bony hands, a broom or a damp cloth. She pulls our ears and catches us by the hair.

Other people also hit and kick us, we don't even know why.

The blows hurt and make us cry.

Falls, scratches, cuts, work, cold and heat can also cause pain.

We decide to toughen our bodies in order to be able to bear pain without crying.

We start by hitting and then punching one another. Seeing our swollen faces, Grandmother asks:

'Who did that to you?'

'We did, Grandmother.'

'You had a fight? Why?'

'For nothing, Grandmother. Don't worry, it's only an exercise.'

'An exercise? You're crazy! Oh well, if that's your idea of fun . . .'

We are naked. We hit one another with a belt. At each blow we say:

'It doesn't hurt.'

We hit harder, harder and harder.

We put our hands over a flame, we cut our thighs, our arms and chests with a knife and pour alcohol on to our wounds. Each time we say:

'It doesn't hurt.'

After a while, in fact, we no longer feel anything. It's someone else who is hurt, someone else who gets burnt, cut and feels pain.

We don't cry any more.

When Grandmother is angry and shouts at us, we say:

'Stop shouting, Grandmother, hit us instead.'

When she hits us, we say:

'More, Grandmother! Look, we are turning the other cheek, as it is written in the Bible. Strike the other cheek, Grandmother.'

She answers:

'May the devil take you with your Bible and your cheeks!'

The Batman

We are lying on the corner seat in the kitchen. Our heads are touching. We aren't asleep yet, but our eyes are shut. Someone pushes the door open. We open our eyes. We are blinded by the light from a torch. We ask:

'Who's there?'

A man's voice answers:

'No fear. You no fear. Two you are, or I too much drink?'

He laughs, lights the oil lamp on the table and turns out his torch. We can see him properly now. He's a foreign soldier, a private. He says:

'I batman of captain. You do what, there?'

We say:

'We live here, it's Grandmother's house.'

'You grandchildren of Witch? I never before see you. You be here since when?'

'For two weeks.'

'Ah! I go on leave my home, in my village. Laugh much.'

We ask:

'How is it you can speak our language?'

He says:

'My mother born here, in your country. Come to work in our country, waitress in café. Meet my father, marry with. When I small, my mother speak me your language. Your country and my country, be friends. Fight the enemy together. You two come from where?'

'From the Big Town.'

'Big Town, much danger. Bang! Bang!'

'Yes, and nothing left to eat.'

'Here, good to eat. Apples, pigs, chickens, everything. You stay long time? Or only holidays?'

'We shall stay until the end of the war.'

'War soon end. You sleep there? Seat bare, hard, cold. Witch no want to take you in room?'

'We don't want to sleep in Grandmother's room. She snores and smells. We had blankets and sheets, but she sold them.'

The batman takes some hot water from the cauldron on the stove and says:

'I must clean room. Captain also return leave tonight or tomorrow morning.'

He goes out. A few minutes later, he comes back. He brings us two grey army blankets.

'No sell that, old Witch. If she be too cruel, you tell me. I, bang, bang, I kill.'

He laughs again. He covers us up, turns out the lamp and goes out.

During the day we hide the blankets in the attic.

Exercise to Toughen the Mind

Grandmother says: 'Sons of a bitch!'

People say to us:

'Sons of a Witch! Sons of a whore!'

Others say:

'Idiots! Hooligans! Filthy kids! Asses! Dirty pups! Pigs! Little devils! Bastards! Little squirts! Gallows birds!'

When we hear these words, our faces get red, our ears buzz, our eyes hurt, our knees tremble.

We don't want to blush or tremble any more, we want to get used to abuse, to hurtful words.

We sit down at the kitchen table opposite one another and, looking each other in the eyes, we say more and more terrible words. One of us says:

'Shit! Arse-hole!'

The other one says:

'Bugger! Sod!'

We go on like this until the words no longer reach our brains, no longer reach even our ears.

We exercise in this way for about half an hour a day, then we go out walking in the streets.

We so arrange matters that people insult us and we note that we have now reached the stage when we don't care any more.

But there are also the old words.

Mother used to say to us:

'My darlings! My loves! My joy! My adorable little babies!'

When we remember these words, our eyes fill with tears.

We must forget these words because, now, nobody says such words to us and because our memory of them is too heavy a burden to bear.

So we begin our exercise again in a different way.

We say:

'My darlings! My loves! I love you . . . I shall never leave you . . . I shall never love anyone but you . . . Forever . . . You are all I have in life . . .'

By repeating them we make these words gradually lose their meaning and the pain that they carry in them is reduced.

School

What follows happened three years ago.

It's evening. Our parents think we are asleep. They are talking about us in the other room.

Mother says:

'They won't bear being separated.'

Father says:

'They'll only be separated during school hours.'

Mother says:

'They won't bear it.'

They'll have to. It's necessary for them. Everybody says so. The teachers, the psychologists, everybody. It will be difficult at first, but they'll get used to it.'

Mother says:

'No, never. I know. I know them. They are one and the same person.'

Father raises his voice:

'Precisely, it isn't normal. They think together. They act together. They live in a different world. In a world of their own. It isn't very healthy. It's even rather worrying. Yes, they worry me. They're odd. You never know what they might be thinking. They're too advanced for their age. They know too much.'

Mother laughs:

'You're not going to criticize them for being too intelligent, I hope?'

'It isn't funny. Why do you laugh?'

Mother replies:

'Twins are always a problem. It isn't the end of the world. Everything will sort itself out.'

Father says:

'Yes, everything will sort itself out if we separate them. Every individual must have his own life.'

A few days later, we start school. We're in different classes. We both sit in the front row.

We are separated from one another by the whole length of the building. This distance between us seems monstrous, the pain is unbearable. It is as if they had taken half our bodies away. We have lost our sense of balance. We feel dizzy, we fall, we lose consciousness.

We wake up in an ambulance taking us to hospital.

Mother comes to fetch us. She smiles and says:

'You'll be in the same class from tomorrow.'

At home, Father just says to us:

'Shammers!'

Soon he leaves for the front. He's a journalist, a war correspondent.

We go to school for two and a half years. The teachers also go away to the front; they are replaced by women teachers. Later, the school closes because there are too many air raids.

We have learnt reading, writing and arithmetic.

At Grandmother's we decide to continue our studies without a teacher, by ourselves.

We Buy Paper, a Notebook and Pencils

At Grandmother's there is no paper, there are no pencils. We go to get some at the shop called Booksellers and Stationers. We choose a packet of squared paper, two pencils and a big, thick notebook. We place all that on the counter in front of the fat gentleman standing on the other side. We say to him:

'We need these things, but we have no money.'

The bookseller says:

'What? But . . . you have to pay.'

We repeat:

'We have no money, but we absolutely need these things.'

The bookseller says:

'The school is shut. Nobody needs notebooks or pencils.'

We say:

'We are having school at home. Just ourselves.'

'Ask your parents for money.'

'Father is at the front and Mother has stayed in the Big Town. We live at our grandmother's, she doesn't have any money either.'

The bookseller says:

'Without money you can't buy anything.'

We don't say anything else, we just look at him. He looks at us, too. His forehead is damp with sweat. After a while he shouts:

'Don't look at me like that! Get out!'

We say:

'We are quite willing to perform certain tasks for you in exchange for these things. We could water or weed your garden, for example, carry parcels . . .'

He shouts again:

'I don't have a garden! I don't need you! And, to begin with, can't you talk normally?'

'We do talk normally.'

'Is it normal, at your age, to say "quite willing to perform certain tasks"?'

'We speak correctly.'

'Too correctly, yes. I don't care at all for the way you talk! Nor for your way of looking at me! Get out!'

We ask:

'Do you have any chickens, sir?'

He dabs his white face with a white handkerchief. He asks, without shouting:

'Chickens? Why chickens?'

'Because if you don't have any, we have at our disposal a certain quantity of eggs and can supply you with them in exchange for these things, which are indispensable to us.'

The bookseller looks at us and says nothing.

We say:

'The price of eggs increases day by day. On the other hand, the price of paper and pencils . . .'

He throws our paper, our pencils and our notebook in the direction of the door and yells:

'Get out! I don't need your eggs! Take all that, and don't come back!'

We carefully pick up the things and say:

'However, we shall be obliged to come back when we have used up all the paper and pencils.'

Our Studies

For our studies we have Father's dictionary and the Bible that we found here, at Grandmother's, in the attic.

We have lessons in spelling, composition, reading, mental arithmetic, mathematics and learning by heart.

We use the dictionary for spelling, to obtain explanations, but also to learn new words, synonyms and antonyms.

We use the Bible for reading aloud, dictation and learning by heart. We are therefore learning whole pages of the Bible by heart.

This is how a composition lesson takes place:

We are sitting at the kitchen table, with our squared sheets of paper, our pencils and the Big Notebook. We're alone.

One of us says:

'The title of your composition is: "Arrival at Grandmother's".'

The other says:

'The title of your composition is: "Our Tasks".'

We start writing. We have two hours to write about the subject and two sheets of paper at our disposal.

At the end of two hours we exchange our sheets of paper, each of us corrects the other's spelling mistakes with the help of the dictionary and, at the bottom of the page, writes: 'Good' or 'Not good'. If it's 'Not good', we throw the composition in the fire and try to write about the same subject in the next lesson. If it's 'Good', we can copy out the composition into the Big Notebook.

To decide whether it is 'Good' or 'Not good', we have a very simple rule: the composition must be true. We must describe what is, what we see, what we hear, what we do.

For example, it is forbidden to write: 'Grandmother is like a witch', but we are allowed to write: 'People call Grandmother the Witch.'

It is forbidden to write: 'The Little Town is beautiful', because the Little Town may be beautiful for us and ugly for someone else.

Similarly, if we write: 'The batman is nice,' this isn't a truth, because the batman may be capable of nasty acts that we know nothing about. So we would simply write: 'The batman has given us some blankets.'

We would write: 'We eat a lot of walnuts' and not: 'We love walnuts', because the word 'love' is not a definite word, it lacks precision and objectivity. 'To love walnuts' and 'to love Mother' don't mean the same thing. The first expression designates a pleasant taste in the mouth, the second a feeling.

Words that define feelings are very vague; it is better to avoid using them and to stick to the description of objects, human beings and oneself; that is to say, to the faithful description of facts.

Our Neighbour and Her Daughter

Our neighbour is not as old as Grandmother. She lives with her daughter in the end house of the Little Town. It is a completely dilapidated building and there are several holes in the roof. Around it there is a garden, but it is not cultivated like Grandmother's garden. Only weeds grow in it.

The neighbour spends all day sitting on a stool in her garden looking straight in front of her. What she is looking at we don't know. In the evenings or when it rains, her daughter takes her by the arm and leads her indoors. Sometimes her daughter forgets her or isn't there, so the mother then spends the whole night out of doors, whatever the weather.

People say that our neighbour is mad, that she went mad when the man who gave her the child abandoned her.

Grandmother says that the neighbour is simply lazy and prefers to stay poor rather than get down to work.

The neighbour's daughter is no taller than us, but she is a bit older. During the day, she begs in the town, outside cafés and at street corners. At the market, she picks up vegetables and rotten fruit that people throw away and takes them home. She also steals what she can. Several times we have had to chase her out of our garden when she was trying to take fruit and eggs.

Once, we catch her drinking milk by sucking the udder of one of our goats.

When she sees us, she gets up, wipes her mouth on the back of her hand, steps back and says:

'Don't hurt me!'

She adds:

'I run very fast. You won't catch me.'

We look at her. It's the first time we have seen her close to. She has a harelip, she is cross-eyed, she has snot in her nose and, in the corner of her red eyes, yellow dirt. Her legs and arms are covered with pimples.

She says:

'I'm called Harelip. I like milk.'

She smiles. Her teeth are black.

'I like milk, but what I like more than anything is sucking the udder. It's good. It's hard and soft at the same time.'

We say nothing. She comes up to us.

'I like to suck something else, too.'

She stretches out her hand. We move back. She says:

'Don't you want to? Don't you want to play with me? I'd like to very much. You are so beautiful.'

She lowers her head and says:

'I disgust you.'

We say:

'No, you don't disgust us.'

'I see. You're too young, too shy. But you don't have to be embarrassed with me. I'll teach you some very amusing games.'

We say:

'We never play.'

'What do you do, then, all day long?'

'We work and study.'

'I beg, steal and play.'

'You also look after your mother. You're a good girl.'

She comes up to us and says:

'You think I'm a good girl? Really?'

'Yes. And if you need anything for your mother or for yourself, you have only to ask us. We'll give you fruit, vegetables, fish and milk.'

She starts shouting:

'I don't want your fruit, your fish or your milk! I can steal all that. What I want is for you to love me. Nobody loves me. Not even my mother. But I don't love anybody either. Neither my mother nor you! I hate you!'

Exercise in Begging

We put on dirty, torn clothes, take off our shoes, dirty our faces and hands. We go out into the street. We stop and wait.

When a foreign officer comes by, we raise our right hands to salute him and hold out our left hands. Usually the officer walks on without seeing us, without looking at us.

In the end, an officer stops. He says something in a language we don't understand. He asks us questions. We don't answer. We stand motionless, one arm raised, the other held out. Then he fumbles in his pockets, places a coin and a bit of chocolate in our dirty hands and goes off, shaking his head.

We go on waiting.

A woman passes by. We hold out our hands. She says:

'Poor kids. I've nothing to give you.'

She strokes our hair.

We say:

'Thank you.'

Another woman gives us two apples, another some biscuits.

A woman passes by. We hold out our hands. She stops and says:

'Aren't you ashamed to beg? Come with me, I've a few easy little jobs for you. Cutting wood, for example, and cleaning up the terrace. You're big enough and strong enough for that. Afterwards, if you work well, I'll give you some bread and soup.'

We answer:

'We don't want to work for you, madam. We don't want to eat your soup or bread. We aren't hungry.'

She asks:

'Why are you begging, then?'

'To find out what effect it has and to observe people's reactions.'

She walks on, shouting:

'Dirty little hooligans! And cheeky with it!'

On our way home, we throw away the apples, biscuits and coins in the tall grass at the roadside.

It is impossible to throw away the stroking on our hair.

Harelip

We are fishing in the stream. Harelip runs up. She doesn't see us. She lies down in the grass and lifts her skirt. She isn't wearing knickers. We see her bare buttocks and the hair between her legs. We don't have hair between our legs. Harelip has some, but not very much.

Harelip whistles. A dog arrives. It's our dog. She takes him in her arms and rolls with him in the grass. The dog barks, gets away, shakes himself and runs off. Harelip calls him gently as she strokes her sex with her fingers.

The dog comes back, sniffs Harelip's sex several times and starts to lick it.

Harelip spreads her legs and presses the dog's head on to her belly with both hands. She breathes very deeply and wriggles.

The dog's sex becomes visible, it gets longer and longer, it is thin and red. The dog raises his head and tries to climb on to Harelip.

Harelip turns round, she is on her knees, she offers her backside to the dog. The dog places his front paws on Harelip's back. His back legs begin to shake. He feels around, gets closer and closer, puts himself between Harelip's legs and sticks himself against her buttocks. He moves very quickly backwards and forwards. Harelip gives a cry and, after a while, she falls on to her stomach.

The dog walks off slowly.

Harelip lies on the ground for a time, then gets up, sees us and blushes. She shouts:

'Dirty little spies! What did you see?'

We answer:

'We saw you playing with our dog.'

She asks:

'Am I still your playmate?'

'Yes. And we'll allow you to play with our dog as much as you like.'

'And you won't tell anybody what you saw?'

'We never tell anybody anything. You can depend on us.'

She sits down in the grass and cries:

'Only animals love me.'

We ask:

'Is it true your mother is mad?'

'No. She's just deaf and blind.'

'What happened to her?'

'Nothing. Nothing special. One day, she went blind and, later on, she went deaf. She says it'll be the same for me. Have you seen my eyes? In the morning, when I wake up, my eyelashes are stuck together and my eyes are full of pus.'

We say:

'It's certainly an illness that can be cured by medicine.'

She says:

'Perhaps. But how can you go to a doctor without any money? Anyway, there aren't any doctors. They're all at the front.'

We ask:

'And what about your ears? Do they hurt?'

'No, I don't have any problem with my ears. And I don't think my mother has either. She pretends not to hear anything; that suits her when I ask her questions.'

Exercise in Blindness and Deafness

One of us pretends to be blind, the other deaf. To begin with, by way of training, the blind one ties one of Grandmother's black shawls over his eyes and the deaf one blocks up his ears with grass. The shawl smells bad, like Grandmother.

We hold hands and go out walking after an air-raid warning has sounded, when people are hiding in their cellars and the streets are deserted.

The deaf one describes what he sees:

'The street is long and straight. It is bordered with low, single-storey houses. They have been painted white, grey, pink, yellow and blue. At the end of the street, I can see a park with trees and a fountain. The sky is blue, with a few white clouds. I can see planes. Five bombers. They are flying low.'

The blind one talks slowly so that the deaf one can lip-read:

'I can hear the planes. They are making a low, jerky noise. Their engines are labouring. They are full of bombs. Now they've passed over. I can hear the birds again. Otherwise everything is quiet.'

The deaf one reads the blind one's lips and answers:

'Yes, the street is empty.'

The blind one says:

'Not for long. I can hear footsteps in the side street on the left.'

The deaf one says:

'You're right. It's a man.'

The blind one asks:

'What is he like?'

The deaf one answers:

'Like all of them. Poor, old.'

The blind one says:

'I know. I recognize old men's footsteps. I can also hear that he is barefoot, so he is poor.'

The deaf one says:

'He's bald. He's wearing an old army jacket. His trousers are too short. His feet are dirty.'

'What about his eyes?'

'I can't see them. He's looking down.'

'And his mouth?'

'His lips are too pulled in. He must have lost all his teeth.'

'And his hands?'

'They're in his pockets. The pockets are huge and filled with something. Potatoes, or walnuts, there are bumps sticking out. He looks up, he's looking at us. But I can't make out the colour of his eyes.'

'Can you see anything else?'

'Lines, deep lines on his face, like scars.'

The blind one says:

'I can hear the all-clear. The raid is over. Let's go home.'

Later, in time, we no longer need a shawl over our eyes or grass in our ears. The one playing the blind man simply turns his gaze inwards and the deaf one shuts his ears off to all sounds.

The Deserter

We find a man in the forest. A living man, a young man, without a uniform. He is lying behind a bush. He looks at us without moving.

We ask him:

'Why are you lying there?'

He answers:

'I can't walk. I've come from the other side of the frontier. I've been walking for two weeks. Night and day. Especially night. I'm too weak now. I'm hungry. I haven't eaten for three days.'

We ask:

'Why haven't you got a uniform? All young men have a uniform. They are all soldiers.'

He says:

'I don't want to be a soldier any more.'

'You don't want to fight the enemy any more?'

'I don't want to fight anyone. I have no enemies. I want to go home.'

'Where is your home?'

'Still a long way off. I'll never get there if I don't find anything to eat.'

We ask:

'Why don't you go and buy something to eat? Haven't you any money?'

'No, I haven't any money and I can't be seen. I must hide. No one must see me.'

'Why?'

'I left my regiment without leave. I ran away. I'm a deserter. If they found me, I'd be shot or hanged.'

We ask:

'Like a murderer?'

'Yes, exactly like a murderer.'

'And yet you don't want to kill anyone. You just want
to go home.'

'Yes, I just want to go home.'

We ask:

'What do you want us to bring you to eat?'

'Anything.'

'Goat's milk, hard-boiled eggs, bread, fruit?'

'Yes, yes, anything.'

We ask:

'And a blanket? The nights are cold and if often rains.'

He says:

'Yes, but you mustn't be seen. And you won't say anything to anybody, will you? Not even to your mother.'

We answer:

'No one will see us, we never say anything to anybody
and we have no mother.'

When we come back with the food and blanket, he says:

'You're very kind.'

We say:

'We didn't want to be kind. We have brought you the
things because you absolutely need them. That's all.'

He says again:

'I don't know how to thank you. I shall never forget
you.'

His eyes fill with tears.

We say:

'Crying is no use, you know. We never cry. Yet we aren't
men, like you.'

He smiles and says:

'You're right. Excuse me, I won't do it any more. It's just because I'm exhausted.'

Exercise in Fasting

We announce to Grandmother:

'Today and tomorrow we won't eat anything. We'll drink only water.'

She shrugs her shoulders:

'I couldn't care less. But you'll work as usual.'

'Of course, Grandmother.'

On the first day, she kills a chicken and roasts it in the oven. At midday, she calls out to us: 'Come and eat!'

We go to the kitchen; it smells very good. We're a bit hungry, but not too much. We watch Grandmother carve up the chicken. She says:

'It smells good. Can you smell how good it smells? Do you want a leg each?'

'We don't want anything, Grandmother.'

'That's a pity, because it is really very good.'

She eats with her hands, licking her fingers and wiping them on her apron. She gnaws and sucks the bones.

She says:

'Very tender, this young chicken. I can't imagine anything better.'

We say:

'Grandmother, ever since we have been in your house, you have never cooked a chicken for us.'

She says:

'I've cooked one today. Now's your chance.'

'You knew we didn't want to eat anything today, or tomorrow.'

'That's not my fault. This is just another of your stupidities.'

'It's one of our exercises. To get us used to bearing hunger.'

'Then get used to it. Nobody's stopping you.'

We go out of the kitchen and go out to do our jobs in the garden. By the end of the day, we are really very hungry. We drink a lot of water. In the evening, we find it hard to get to sleep. We dream of food.

Next day, at midday, Grandmother finishes the chicken. We watch her eating it in a kind of fog. We're no longer hungry. We feel dizzy.

In the evening, Grandmother makes pancakes, which she serves with jam and cream cheese. We feel sick and have stomach cramps but, as soon as we get into bed, we fall into a deep sleep. When we get up, Grandmother has already left for the market. We want to have our breakfast, but there is nothing to eat in the kitchen. No bread, no milk, no cheese. Grandmother has locked everything away in the cellar. We could unlock it, but we decide not to touch anything. We eat raw tomatoes and cucumbers with salt.

Grandmother comes back from the market and says:

'You haven't done your work this morning.'

'You should have woken us, Grandmother.'

'You should have woken yourselves up. But, just this once, I'll give you something to eat all the same.'

She makes us a vegetable soup with what she brings back from the market, as usual. We don't have much of it. After the meal, Grandmother says:

'It's a stupid exercise. And bad for the health.'

Grandfather's Grave

One day, we see Grandmother leave the house with her watering-can and gardening tools. But instead of going to the vineyard she goes in a different direction. We follow her at a distance in order to find out where she is going.

She goes into the graveyard. She stops in front of a grave and puts down her tools. The graveyard is deserted. There is nobody but Grandmother and us.

Hiding behind bushes and funerary monuments, we get closer and closer. Grandmother is short-sighted and poor of hearing. We can observe her without her knowing.

She pulls up the weeds growing on the grave, digs with a spade, rakes the soil, plants flowers, fetches water from the well and comes back and waters the grave.

When she has finished her work, she gathers her tools together, then kneels down in front of the wooden cross, but sitting back on her heels. She joins her hands over her belly as if to say a prayer, but what we hear are mainly oaths:

'Shit . . . bastard . . . pig . . . rotten . . . damned . . .'

When Grandmother has gone, we go and look at the grave: it is very well maintained. We look at the cross: the name written on it is our grandmother's. It is also Mother's maiden name. The Christian name is double, with a hyphen, and those two Christian names are our Christian names.

On the cross, there are also dates of birth and death. We calculate that Grandfather died at the age of forty-four, twenty-three years ago.

In the evening, we ask Grandmother:

'What was our Grandfather like?'

She says:

'What? You don't have a grandfather.'

'But we used to have.'

'No, never. He had already died when you were born. So you never had a grandfather.'

We ask:

'Why did you poison him?'

She asks:

'What are you talking about?'

'People say you poisoned Grandfather.'

'People say . . . People say . . . Let them tell their stories.'

'You didn't poison him?'

'Leave me alone, sons of a bitch! Nothing was proved! People say anything.'

We say again:

'We know you didn't like Grandfather. So why do you look after his grave?'

'For that very reason! Because of what people say. To stop them telling their stories! And how do you know I look after his grave, eh? You've been spying on me, sons of a bitch, you've been spying on me again! May the devil take you!'

Exercise in Cruelty

It's Sunday. We catch a chicken and cut its throat as we have seen Grandmother do. We bring the chicken into the kitchen and say:

'You must cook it, Grandmother.'

She starts shouting:

'Who gave you permission? You've no right! I give the orders here, you filthy kids! I won't cook it! I'd rather die first!'

We say:

'All right. We'll cook it ourselves.'

We start to pluck the chicken, but Grandmother snatches it from our hands.

'You don't know how to do it! Filthy little kids, you'll be the death of me, you're God's punishment on me, that's what you are!'

As the chicken is cooking, Grandmother cries:

'It was the best one. They took the best one on purpose. It was just ready for the Tuesday market.'

As we eat the chicken we say:

'It's very good, this chicken. We'll eat chicken every Sunday.'

'Every Sunday? Are you crazy? Do you want to ruin me?'

'We shall eat a chicken every Sunday, whether you like it or not.'

Grandmother starts to cry:

'But what have I done to them? Woe is me! They want to

kill me. A poor, old defenceless woman, I haven't deserved this. And I've been so good to them!'

'Yes, Grandmother, you are good, very good. So it is out of kindness that you will cook a chicken for us every Sunday.'

When she has calmed down a bit, we say to her again:

'When there's something to be killed, you must fetch us. We'll do it.'

She says:

'You like that, eh?'

'No, Grandmother, it's precisely because we don't like it. It's for that reason that we must get used to it.'

She says:

'I see. It's a new exercise. You're right. It's good to know how to kill when you have to.'

We begin with the fish. We pick them up by the tail and bang their heads against a stone. We soon get used to killing the animals intended to be eaten: chickens, rabbits, ducks. Later, we will kill animals which do not need to be killed. We catch frogs, nail them down on a piece of wood and slit their bellies open. We also catch butterflies and pin them on to a piece of cardboard. Soon we have a fine collection.

One day we hang our cat, a ginger tom-cat, from the branch of a tree. As he hangs, he gets longer and becomes enormous. He has spasms and convulsions. When he isn't moving any more, we cut him down. He lies stretched out on the grass, motionless, then, suddenly, gets up and runs off.

Ever since then, he no longer comes near the house, but we sometimes see him at a distance. He doesn't even come to drink the milk that we put out in front of the door on a little plate.

Grandmother says:

'That cat is getting wilder and wilder.'

We say:

'Don't worry, Grandmother, we'll take care of the mice.'

We make traps and drown the mice that get caught in them in boiling water.

The Other Children

We meet other children in the Little Town. As the school is shut, they are out all day long. There are big ones and little ones. Some have their homes and mothers here, others are from elsewhere, like us. Especially from the Big Town.

A lot of these children are living with people they didn't know before. They have to work in the fields and vineyards; the people who look after them are not always very kind to them.

The big children often attack the small ones. They take all they have in their pockets and sometimes they even take their clothes. They beat them up, too, especially those who come from elsewhere. The young ones who are from here are protected by their mothers and never go out alone.

We are not protected by anybody, so we learn to defend ourselves against the big ones.

We make weapons: we sharpen stones, we fill socks with sand and gravel. We also have a razor, which we found in the chest in the attic, next to the Bible. We have only to take out our razor for the big boys to run away.

On one very hot day, we are sitting beside the fountain where people who have no well of their own come and get water. Nearby, some boys who are bigger than us are lying in the grass. It is cool there, under the trees, near the water, which runs without stopping.

Harelip arrives with a bucket, which she places under

the spout, out of which a thin trickle of water comes. She waits for her bucket to be filled.

When the bucket is full, one of the boys gets up and goes and spits in it. Harelip empties the bucket, rinses it and puts it back under the spout.

When the bucket is full again, another boy gets up and goes and spits in it. Harelip puts the rinsed bucket back under the spout. She doesn't wait for the bucket to be full. She fills it only one half full and quickly tries to get away.

One of the boys runs after her, catches her by the arm and spits into the bucket.

Harelip says:

'Stop it, will you? I have to take clean drinking water back.'

The boy says:

'But the water is clean, I've just spat in it. You're not saying my spit is dirty, I hope! My spit is cleaner than anything in your house!'

Harelip empties her bucket and cries.

The boy opens his flies and says:

'Suck it! If you suck me off, we'll let you fill your bucket.'

Harelip kneels down. The boy steps back:

'Do you think I'm going to put my cock into your disgusting mouth? Filthy cow!'

He kicks Harelip in the chest and does up his flies.

We go over. We pick Harelip up, take her bucket, rinse it well and put it under the fountain spout.

One of the boys says to the other two:

'Come on, let's be off.'

Another says:

'Are you crazy, this is where the fun starts.'

The first one says:

'Drop it! I know them. They're dangerous.'

'Dangerous? Those little cunts? I'll take care of them, you'll see.'

He comes up to us, makes to spit in the bucket, but one of us trips him up, while the other hits him on the head with a bag of sand. The boy falls down. He lies on the ground, knocked out. The other two look at us. One of them moves towards us. The other says:

'Watch out! Those little bastards are capable of anything. Once they split my temple open with a stone. They've got a razor, too, and they don't hesitate to use it. They'd slit your throat as soon as look at you. They're completely crazy.'

The boys go off.

We hand the filled bucket to Harelip. She asks us:

'Why didn't you help me right away?'

'We wanted to see how you defended yourself.'

'What would I have been able to do against three big lads?'

'Throw your bucket at their heads, scratch their faces, kick them in the balls, shout and yell, or run off and come back later.'

Winter

It's getting colder and colder. We rummage in our suit-cases and put on almost everything we can find: several pullovers, several pairs of trousers. But we can't put on a second pair of shoes over our worn-out town shoes, which have holes in them. Anyway, we don't have any others. Nor do we have any gloves or hats. Our hands and feet are covered with chilblains.

The sky is dark grey, the streets in the town are emp-ty, the stream is frozen, the forest is covered with snow. We can't go out to it any more. So we'll soon be without wood.

We say to Grandmother:

'We need two pairs of gumboots.'

She answers:

'And what else do you need? Where do you expect me to find the money?'

'Grandmother, there's hardly any wood left.'

'Then we'll have to go easy on it.'

We don't go out any more. We do all kinds of exercises, we carve various objects out of wood, like spoons and breadboards, and we study late into the night. Grand-mother spends almost all the time in bed. She hardly ever goes into the kitchen. We are left in peace.

We eat badly; there are no more vegetables and fruit, the hens aren't laying any more. Every day Grandmother brings up some dried beans and a few potatoes from the cellar, which is full of smoked meats and jars of jam.

The postman comes sometimes. He rings his bicycle bell until Grandmother comes out of the house. He then moistens his pencil, writes something on a bit of paper and hands the pencil and paper to Grandmother, who puts a cross at the bottom of the paper. The postman gives her some money, a packet or a letter and goes off in the direction of the town, whistling.

Grandmother locks herself in her room with the parcel or the money. If there's a letter, she throws it into the fire.

We ask:

'Grandmother, why do you throw the letter away without reading it?'

She answers:

'I can't read. I never went to school. I've never done anything but work. I wasn't spoilt like you.'

'We could read you the letters you get.'

'Nobody must read the letters I get.'

We ask:

'Who sends the money? Who sends you parcels? Who sends you letters?'

She doesn't answer.

Next day, while she is in the cellar, we search her room. Under the bed, we find an open parcel. In it there are pullovers, scarves, hats and gloves. We say nothing to Grandmother, because if we did she would realize that we have a key to her room.

After the evening meal, we wait. Grandmother drinks her brandy, then staggers over to open her bedroom door holding the key that hangs from her belt. We follow her and push her from behind. She falls on to her bed. We pretend to look for something and find the parcel.

We say:

'That's not very nice, Grandmother. We're cold, we have

no warm clothes, we can no longer go out and you want to sell everything Mother has knitted and sent for us.'

Grandmother says nothing, she cries.

We say again:

'It's Mother who sends money, Mother who writes you letters.'

Grandmother says:

'It isn't to me she writes. She knows very well I can't read. She never used to write to me. Now you're here, she writes. But I don't need her letters! I don't need anything that comes from her!'

The Postman

From now on we wait for the postman in front of the garden gate. He's an old man with a cap. He has a bicycle with two leather pouches attached to the parcel-rack.

When he arrives, we don't give him time to ring: very quickly we unscrew his bell.

He says:

'Where's your grandmother?'

We say:

'Don't worry about her. Give us what you have brought.'

He says:

'There's nothing.'

He tries to get away, but we give him a push. He falls into the snow. His bicycle falls on top of him. He swears.

We search his pouches and find a letter and a postal order. We take the letter and say:

'Give us the money!'

He says:

'No. It's addressed to your grandmother.'

We say:

'But it's intended for us. It has been sent to us by our mother. If you don't hand it over, we'll stop you getting up until you die of cold.'

He says:

'All right, all right. Help me get up, one of my legs is crushed under the bike.'

We pick up the bicycle and help the postman to get up.

He is very thin, very light.

He takes the money out of one of his pockets and gives it to us.

We ask:

'Do you want a signature or a cross?'

He says:

'A cross will do. One cross is as good as another.'

He adds:

'You're right to defend yourselves. Everybody knows what your grandmother's like. There's nobody meaner than her. So it's your mother who sends you all that? She's very nice. I knew her when she was a little girl. She did well to leave here. She would never have been able to marry here. With all the stories . . .'

We ask:

'What stories?'

'Like how she was supposed to have poisoned her husband. I mean, your grandmother poisoned your grandfather. It's an old story. That's why they call her the Witch.'

We say:

'We don't want anyone to speak ill of Grandmother.'

The postman turns his bicycle round:

'All right, all right, but you ought to be kept informed.'

We say:

'We were already informed. From now on you will give the mail to us. Otherwise we'll kill you. Understand?'

The postman says:

'You'd be quite capable of it, you've the makings of murderers. You'll have your mail, I don't care. I couldn't care less about the Witch.'

He leaves, pushing his bicycle. He drags his leg to show that we hurt him.

Next day, warmly dressed, we go off to town to buy gumboots with the money that Mother has sent us. We take turns to carry her letter under our shirts.

The Cobbler

The cobbler lives and works in the basement of a house near the station. The room is enormous. In one corner there is his bed, in another his kitchen. His workshop is in front of the window, which is at ground level. The cobbler is sitting on a low stool surrounded by shoes and tools. He looks at us over his spectacles; he looks at our cracked patent-leather shoes.

We say:

'Good morning. We would like warm, waterproof gum-boots. Do you sell any? We have money.'

He says:

'Yes, I sell them. But the lined ones, the warm ones, are very expensive.'

We say:

'We absolutely need them. Our feet are cold.'

We put what money we have on the low table.

The cobbler says:

'It's just enough for one pair. But one pair will be enough for you. You're the same size. Each of you can go out in turn.'

'That isn't possible. One of us never goes out without the other. We go everywhere together.'

'Ask your parents for more money, then.'

'We have no parents. We live with our grandmother, whom they call the Witch. She won't give us any money.'

The cobbler says:

'The Witch is your grandmother? Poor kids! And you've

come from her house to here in those shoes!'

'Yes, we have. We can't get through the winter without boots. We have to go into the forest to fetch wood; we have to clear the snow. We absolutely need . . .'

'Two pairs of warm, waterproof boots.'

The cobbler laughs and hands us two pairs of boots:

'Try them on.'

We try them on; they fit us very well.

We say:

'We'll keep them. We'll pay you for the second pair in the spring when we sell fish and eggs. Or, if you prefer, we'll bring you wood.'

The cobbler hands us back our money:

'Here, take it. I don't want your money. Buy yourselves some good socks with it. I'll give you the boots because you absolutely need them.'

We say:

'We don't like to accept presents.'

'And why not?'

'Because we don't like to say thank you.'

'Nobody's making you say anything. Be off with you. No. Wait a moment! Take these slippers, too, and these sandals for the summer and these shoes, too, they're very strong. Take whatever you like.'

'But why are you giving us all these things?'

'I don't need them any more. I'll be going away soon.'

We ask:

'Where are you going to?'

'Who knows? They'll take me away and kill me.'

We ask:

'Who wants to kill you, and why?'

He says:

'Don't ask questions. Be off with you now.'

We pick up the shoes, the slippers and the sandals. We have the boots on our feet. We stop in front of the door and say:

'We hope they won't take you away. Or, if they do take you away, we hope they won't kill you. Goodbye, sir, and thank you, thank you very much.'

When we get back, Grandmother asks:

'Where did you steal all that, you gallows-birds?'

'We didn't steal any of it. It's a present. Not everybody is as mean as you, Grandmother.'

The Theft

With our boots and our warm clothes, we can go out once more. We slide on the frozen stream, we go and look for wood in the forest.

We take an axe and a saw with us. We can no longer collect the dead wood lying on the ground; the layer of snow is too thick. We climb up trees, saw off the dead branches and cut them up with the axe. During this work, we aren't cold. We even sweat. So we take off our gloves and put them in our pockets so that they won't get worn too quickly.

One day, coming back with our two bundles of firewood, we make a detour to go and see Harelip.

The snow has not been cleared from in front of the house and there are no footsteps leading to it. There is no smoke coming out of the chimney.

We knock on the door, there is no answer. We go in. At first we see nothing, it is so dark, but our eyes soon get used to the darkness.

It's a room that serves both as kitchen and as bedroom. In the darkest corner, there's a bed. We go up to it. We call out. Someone moves under the blanket and old clothes; Harelip's head emerges.

We ask:

'Is your mother there?'

She says:

'Yes.'

'Is she dead?'

'I don't know.'

We put down our firewood and light a fire in the stove, because it's as cold in the room as outside. Then we go back to Grandmother's and get some potatoes and dried beans from the cellar. We milk one of the goats and come back to our neighbour's. We heat the milk. We melt some snow in a saucepan and cook the beans in it. We bake the potatoes in the oven.

Harelip gets up and totters over to a chair by the fire.

Our neighbour isn't dead. We pour some goat's milk into her mouth. We say to Harelip:

'When all this is ready, eat it and give some to your mother. We'll be back.'

With the money that the cobbler gave us back, we have bought a few pairs of socks but we haven't spent everything. We go into a grocer's to buy some flour and take some salt and sugar without paying for them. We also go to the butcher's; we buy a small slice of bacon and take a big sausage without paying for it. We go back to Harelip's. She and her mother have already eaten everything. The mother is still in bed, Harelip is washing up.

We say to her:

'We'll bring you a bundle of firewood every day. Some beans and potatoes, too. But, for the rest, you need money: We don't have any more. Without money, you can't go into a shop. You have to buy something if you're going to steal something else.'

She says:

'You really are clever. You're right. They don't even let me into the shops. I'd never have thought you were capable of stealing.'

We say:

'Why not? It will be our exercise in skill. But we need a little money. Absolutely.'

She thinks about it and says:

'Go and ask the parish priest. He sometimes used to give me money when I let him see my slit.'

'He asked you that?'

'Yes. And sometimes he put his finger in. And afterwards he gave me money not to tell anybody. Tell him Harelip and her mother need money.'

Blackmail

We go and see the parish priest. He lives next to the church in a big house, which is called the presbytery.

We pull on the bell-pull. An old woman opens the door:

'What do you want?'

'We want to see the parish priest.'

'Why?'

'It's for someone who is going to die.'

The old woman takes us into a waiting room. She knocks on a door:

'Father,' she shouts, 'it's for an extreme unction.'

A voice answers from behind the door:

'I'm coming. Tell them to wait.'

We wait for a few minutes. A tall, thin man with a severe face comes out of the room. He is wearing a sort of white and gold cloak over his dark clothes. He asks us:

'Where is it? Who sent you?'

'Harelip and her mother.'

He says:

'What is the precise name of these people.'

'We don't know their precise name. The mother is blind and deaf. She lives in the end house at the edge of the town. They are dying of hunger and cold.'

The priest says:

'Although I know absolutely nothing about these people, I am willing to give them extreme unction. Let's go. Lead the way.'

We say:

'They don't need extreme unction yet. They need a little money. We've brought them wood, a few potatoes and some dried beans, but we can't do any more. Harelip has sent us here. You used to give her a little money sometimes.'

The priest says:

'It's quite possible. I give money to a lot of poor people. I can't remember all of them. Here!'

He fumbles in his pockets under his cloak and gives us a little money. We take it and say:

'That's not very much. It's too little. It isn't even enough to buy a loaf of bread.'

He says:

'I'm sorry. There are a lot of poor people. And the faithful have almost stopped giving offerings. Everybody is in difficulties at the moment. Off with you now and God bless you!'

We say:

'We can accept this sum for today, but we will have to come back tomorrow.'

'What? What is that supposed to mean? Tomorrow? I shan't let you in. Get out of here immediately.'

'Tomorrow, we will ring the bell until you let us in. We will knock at the windows, we will kick at your door and tell everybody what you did to Harelip.'

'I never did anything to Harelip. I don't even know who she is. She must be making up these things. The stories of a mentally deficient child will not be taken seriously. No one will believe you. Everything she is saying is untrue!'

We say:

'Never mind whether it's true or untrue. The point is it's calumny. People like scandal.'

The priest sits down on a chair and wipes his face with a handkerchief.

'It's monstrous. Have you any idea what you are doing?'

'Yes, sir. Blackmail.'

'At your age . . . It's deplorable.'

'Yes, it's deplorable that we've been forced to this. But Harelip and her mother absolutely need money.'

The priest gets up, takes off his cloak and says:

'It is a trial sent from God. How much do you want? I'm not well off, you know.'

'Ten times what you have already given us. Once a week. We aren't asking you for the impossible.'

He takes the money out of his pocket and gives it to us:

'Come each Saturday. But don't in any way imagine that I'm doing this in order to give in to your blackmail. I'm doing it out of charity.'

We say:

'That's exactly what we expected of you, Father.'

Accusations

One afternoon the batman comes into the kitchen. We haven't seen him for a long time. He says:

'You come help unload Jeep.'

We put on our boots and follow him out to the Jeep, which has stopped on the road, in front of the garden gate. The batman hands us chests and cardboard boxes, which we carry into the officer's room.

We ask:

'Is the officer coming this evening? We've never seen him.'

The batman says:

'Officer no come winter here. Perhaps come never. He unhappy in love. Perhaps he find another later. Forget. Stories like that not for you. You bring wood to heat room.'

We bring wood and make a fire in the small metal stove. The batman opens the chests and boxes and puts on the table bottles of wine, brandy, beer, and a lot of things to eat – sausages, cans of meat and vegetables, rice, biscuits, chocolate, sugar and coffee.

The batman opens a bottle, starts to drink and says:

'I heat food in billy-can on paraffin stove. Tonight eat, drink, sing with friends. Celebrate victory against the enemy. We soon win war with new wonder weapon.'

We ask:

'So the war will soon be over?'

He says:

'Yes, very soon. Why you look like that food on the table? If you are hungry, eat chocolate, biscuits, sausage.'

We say:

'There are people dying of hunger.'

'So what? No think of that. Many people die of hunger or other things. No think. We eat and not die.'

He laughs. We say:

'We know a blind, deaf woman who lives near here with her daughter. They won't survive this winter.'

'It is not my fault.'

'Yes, it is your fault. Yours and your country's. You brought us the war.'

'Before the war, how they do to eat, the blind woman and daughter?'

'Before the war, they lived on charity. People gave them old clothes and shoes. They brought them food. Now nobody gives anything any more. The people are all poor or are afraid of becoming so. The war has made them mean and selfish.'

The batman shouts:

'I no care all that! Enough! Silence!'

'Yes, you don't care and you eat our food.'

'Not your food. I take that in barracks stores.'

'Everything on that table comes from our country: the drink, the canned food, the biscuits, the sugar. Our country feeds your army.'

The batman goes red in the face. He sits down on his bed and holds his head in his hands:

'You think I want war and come to your filthy country? I much better at home, quiet, make chairs and tables. Drink wine of my country, have fun with nice girls at home. Here everybody unkind, you, too, little children. You say all my fault. I what can do? If I say I no go to war, no come in your country, I shot. You take all, go take all on table. Celebration finished. I sad, you too unkind with me.'

We say:

'We don't want to take everything, just a few cans and a little chocolate. But you could bring us, from time to time, at least during the winter, some powdered milk, flour or anything else to eat.'

He says:

'That I can. You come with me tomorrow to blind woman's house. But you nice with me, after. Yes?'

We say:

'Yes.'

The batman laughs. His friends arrive. We leave. We hear them singing all night.

The Priest's Housekeeper

One morning, towards the end of the winter, we are sitting in the kitchen with Grandmother. There is a knock on the door; a young woman comes in.

She says:

'Good morning. I've come for some potatoes for . . .'

She stops speaking and looks at us:

'Why, they're adorable!'

She takes a stool and sits down:

'Come here, you.'

We don't move.

'Or you.'

We don't move. She laughs:

'Come on, come over here. Are you afraid of me?'

We say:

'We're afraid of nobody.'

We go over to her; she says:

'Heavens! How beautiful you are! But how dirty you are!'

Grandmother asks:

'What do you want?'

'Potatoes for the priest. Why are you so dirty? Don't you ever wash?'

Grandmother says angrily:

'It's none of your business. Why didn't the old woman come?'

The young woman laughs again:

'The old woman! She was younger than you. But she

died yesterday. She was my aunt. I'm replacing her at the presbytery.'

Grandmother says:

'She was five years older than me. She died, just like that? . . . How many potatoes do you want?'

'Ten kilos, or more, if you have them. And some apples. And also . . . what else have you got? The priest is as thin as a rake and he's got nothing in his larder.'

Grandmother says:

'You should have thought of that in the autumn.'

'I wasn't there in the autumn. I've only been there since yesterday evening.'

Grandmother says:

'I'm warning you, at this time of year, all food is very dear.'

The young woman laughs again:

'State your price. We don't have any choice. There's almost nothing left in the shops.'

'Soon there'll be nothing left anywhere.'

Grandmother sniggers and goes out. We are left alone with the priest's housekeeper. She asks us:

'Why don't you ever wash?'

'There's no bathroom, no soap. It isn't possible to wash.'

'And your clothes! What a mess! Haven't you any other clothes?'

'We have some in the suitcases, under the seat, but they're all dirty and torn. Grandmother never washes them.'

'The Witch is your grandmother? Wonders never cease!'

Grandmother comes back with two sacks:

'That'll be ten silver coins or one gold coin. I don't accept notes. They'll soon be worth nothing at all – they're just paper.'

The housekeeper asks:

'What's in the sacks?'

Grandmother answers:

'Food. Take it or leave it.'

'I'll take it. I'll bring you the money tomorrow. Can the two boys help me carry the sacks?'

'They can if they want to. They don't always want to. They don't obey anybody.'

The housekeeper asks us:

'You will do that for me, won't you? You'll each carry a sack and I'll carry your suitcases.'

Grandmother asks:

'What's all this about suitcases?'

'I'm going to wash their dirty clothes. I'll bring them back tomorrow with the money.'

Grandmother sniggers:

'Wash their clothes! Well, if you've nothing better to do . . .'

We go off with the housekeeper. We follow her to the presbytery. We see two long, thick blonde plaits dancing over her black shawl. They reach down to her waist. Her hips dance under her red skirt. We can just see a bit of her legs between the skirt and her boots. Her stockings are black and the one on her right leg has laddered.

The Bath

We arrive at the presbytery with the housekeeper. She lets us in by the back door. We put down the sacks in the larder and go to the wash-house. There are lots of ropes stretched across the room to hold the washing. There are receptacles of every kind, including a zinc bath-tub, of odd shape, like a deep armchair.

The housekeeper opens our suitcases, puts our clothes into cold water to soak, then starts a fire to heat water in two big cauldrons. She says:

'I'll wash straight away what you need at once. While you're bathing, they will dry. I'll bring you the other clothes tomorrow or the day after. They also need mending.'

She pours hot water into the bath-tub; she adds cold water to it:

'Well, who's first?'

We don't move.

She says:

'Who's it going to be, you or you? Come on, get undressed!'

We ask:

'Are you going to stay here while we bathe?'

She laughs very loudly:

'What! Of course I'll stay here! I'll even rub your backs and wash your hair. You're surely not going to be embarrassed in front of me, are you? I'm almost old enough to be your mother.'

We still don't move. Then she starts to undress:

'Oh, well. Then I'll go first. You see, I'm not embarrassed to undress in front of you. You're only little boys.'

She hums to herself, but her face goes red when she realizes that we are staring at her. She has tight, pointed breasts like balloons that have not yet been fully blown up. Her skin is very white and she has a lot of blonde hair everywhere. Not only between her legs and under her arms, but also on her belly and thighs. She goes on singing in the water, rubbing herself with a flannel. When she gets out of the bath, she quickly slips into a bathrobe. She changes the water in the tub and, turning her back to us, starts to do the washing. Then we get undressed and get into the tub together. There's plenty of room for both of us.

After a while, she hands us two large, white cloths:

'I hope you rubbed yourselves well all over.'

We sit down on a bench, wrapped up in our cloths, waiting for our clothes to dry. The wash-house is full of steam and it's very warm. The housekeeper comes up to us holding a pair of scissors:

'Now I'm going to cut your nails. And stop playing about; I won't eat you.'

She cuts our fingernails and our toenails. She also cuts our hair. She kisses us on the face and on the neck; she never stops talking:

'Oh! What pretty little feet, how sweet they are, all clean now! Oh! What adorable ears, what a soft, soft neck! Oh! How I would love to have two pretty, handsome little boys like you, all to myself! I'd tickle them all over, all over, all over.'

She strokes and kisses us all over our bodies. With her tongue she tickles us on our necks, under our arms, between our buttocks. She kneels down in front of the seat and sucks our cocks, which get bigger and harder in her mouth.

She is now sitting between us; she puts her arms around us and presses us to her:

'If I had two pretty little babies like you, I'd give them lovely sweet milk to drink, here, like this.'

She pulls our heads down to her breasts, which are sticking out of her bathrobe, and we suck the pink ends, which become very hard. She puts her hands under her bathrobe and rubs herself between the legs:

'What a pity you aren't older! Oh! How nice it is, how nice it is to play with you!'

She sighs, pants, then, suddenly, stiffens.

As we are leaving, she says to us:

'You'll come back every Saturday to bathe. You'll bring your dirty clothes with you. I want you to be always clean.'

We say:

'We'll bring you wood in exchange for your work. And fish and mushrooms when there are any.'

The Priest

The following Saturday, we go back to have our bath. Afterwards, the housekeeper says to us:

'Come into the kitchen. I'll make some tea and we'll have some bread and butter.'

We are eating the bread and butter when the priest comes into the kitchen.

We say:

'Good morning, sir.'

The housekeeper says:

'Father, these are my two protégés. They're the grandsons of the old woman people call the Witch.'

The priest says:

'Yes, I know them. Come with me.'

We follow him. We cross a room in which there is nothing but a big round table surrounded by chairs and a crucifix on the wall. Then we go into a dark room, where the walls are lined with books from floor to ceiling. Opposite the door, there's a prie-dieu with a crucifix; near the window, a desk, a narrow bed in one corner, three chairs arranged against the wall: that's all the furniture there is in the room.

The priest says:

'You've changed a lot. You're clean. You look like two angels. Sit down.'

He pulls up two chairs opposite his desk; we sit down. He sits down behind his desk. He hands us an envelope:

'Here's the money.'

As we take the envelope, we say:

'You'll soon be able to stop giving them any more. In summer, Harelip manages by herself.'

The priest says:

'No. I shall go on helping these two women. I'm ashamed that I did not do so earlier. And now, let's talk about something else, shall we?'

He looks at us; we say nothing. He says:

'I never see you in church.'

'We don't go there.'

'Do you pray sometimes?'

'No, we don't pray.'

'Poor lost lambs. I shall pray for you. Can you read, at least?'

'Yes, sir. We can read.'

The priest hands us a book:

'Here, read this. You will find in it beautiful stories about Jesus Christ and the lives of the saints.'

'We know these stories already. We have a Bible. We have read the Old Testament and the New.'

The priest raises his dark eyebrows:

'What? You have read the whole of the Holy Bible?'

'Yes, sir. We even know several passages by heart.'

'Which ones, for example?'

'Passages from Genesis, Exodus, Ecclesiastes, The Book of Revelation and others.'

The priest is silent for a while, then he says:

'So you know the Ten Commandments. Do you obey them?'

'No, sir, we do not obey them. Nobody obeys them. It is written "Thou shalt not kill" and everybody kills.'

The priest says:

'Alas . . . it's wartime.'

We say:

'We would like to read other books than the Bible, but we don't have any. You have a lot of books. You could lend us some.'

'These books are too difficult for you.'

'Are they more difficult than the Bible?'

The priest looks at us. He asks:

'What kind of books would you like to read?'

'History books and geography books. Books that tell us true things, not invented things.'

The priest says:

'By next Saturday, I shall find some books that will be suitable for you. Now leave me. Go back to the kitchen and finish your tea.'

The Housekeeper and the Batman

We are picking cherries in the garden with the house-keeper when the batman and the foreign officer arrive in the Jeep. The officer walks straight past us and goes into his room. The batman stops near us and says:

'Good morning, little friends, good morning pretty maiden. Cherries already ripe? I love much cherries, I love much pretty young lady.'

The officer calls out through the window. The batman has to go into the house. The housekeeper says to us:

'Why didn't you tell me there were men in your house?'

'They're foreigners.'

'So what? What a handsome man he is, the officer!'

We ask:

'Don't you like the batman?'

'He's small and fat.'

'But he's nice and amusing. And he speaks our language very well.'

She says:

'I don't care. It's the officer I like.'

The officer comes and sits on the seat in front of the window. The housekeeper's basket is already full of cherries. She could go back to the presbytery, but she stays there. She looks at the officer and laughs very loudly. She hangs from the branch of a tree, she swings, she jumps, she lies in the grass and, finally, she throws a daisy at the officer's feet. The officer gets up and goes into his room. Soon afterwards, he comes out and goes off in his Jeep.

The batman leans out of the window and shouts:

'Who can help poor man clean very dirty room?'

We say:

'We'll help you.'

He says:

'Need a woman to help. Need pretty young lady.'

We say to the housekeeper:

'Come on. Let's help him a bit.'

We all three go into the officer's room. The housekeeper picks up a broom and starts to sweep. The batman sits on the bed and says:

'I dream. A princess, I see in dream. Princess must pinch me to wake me up.'

The housekeeper laughs and pinches the batman's cheek very hard.

The batman shouts:

'I awake now. I also want pinch wicked princess.'

He takes the housekeeper in his arms and pinches her bottom. The housekeeper struggles, but the batman holds her very tight. He says to us:

'You, outside! And shut the door.'

We ask the housekeeper:

'Do you want us to stay?'

She laughs:

'What for? I can look after myself very well.'

So we go out of the room and shut the door behind us. The housekeeper comes to the window, smiles at us, draws the shutters and shuts the window. We go up into the attic and, through the holes, look at what is happening in the officer's room.

The batman and the housekeeper are lying on the bed. The housekeeper is entirely naked; the batman has just his shirt and socks on. He is lying on the housekeeper and both move backwards and forwards and from left to right. The batman moans like Grandmother's pig and the house-keeper cries out, as if in pain, but she also laughs at the same time and says:

'Yes, yes, yes! Oh! Oh! Oh!'

From that day on, the housekeeper often comes back and shuts herself up with the batman. We sometimes look at them, but not always.

The batman prefers the housekeeper to bend over or to squat on all fours, and he takes her from behind.

The housekeeper prefers the batman to lie on his back. She then sits on the batman's belly and moves up and down, as if she was riding a horse.

The batman sometimes gives the housekeeper silk stockings or eau-de-cologne.

The Foreign Officer

We are doing our immobility exercise in the garden. It is warm. We are lying on our backs in the shade of the walnut tree. Through the leaves, we see the sky and the clouds. The leaves of the tree are motionless; the clouds also seem to be but, if we look at them for a long time, very attentively, we notice that they change shape and stretch out.

Grandmother comes out of the house. As she walks past us, she kicks sand and gravel into our faces and over our bodies. She mutters something and goes into the vineyard for her siesta.

The officer is sitting, stripped to the waist, his eyes shut, on the seat in front of his room, his head leaning against the white wall, in full sunlight. Suddenly he comes over to us; he speaks to us, but we don't answer or look at him. He goes back to his seat.

Later, the batman says to us:

'The officer wants you to go and speak to him.'

We don't answer. He says again:

'You get up and come. Officer angry if you not obey.'

We don't move.

The officer says something and the batman goes into the room. We hear him singing as he cleans the room.

When the sun touches the roof of the house, beside the chimney, we get up. We go over to the officer. We stop in front of him. He calls the batman. We ask:

'What does he want?'

The officer asks some questions; the batman translates:

'The officer ask why you not move, why not speak?'

We answer:

'We were doing our immobility exercise.'

The batman translates again:

'The officer say you two do many exercises. Also other kinds. He has seen you hit each other with belt.'

'That was our toughening up exercise.'

'The officer ask why you do all that?'

'To get used to pain.'

'He ask you have pleasure in pain?'

'No. We only want to overcome pain, heat, cold, hunger, whatever causes pain.'

'The officer admiration for you. He find you extraordinary.'

The officer adds a few words. The batman says:

'Good, finished. I must go now. You also go, go fishing.'

But the officer holds us by the arm, smiling, and makes a sign for the batman to go. The batman walks a little way, then turns back:

'You leave! Quick! Go for walk in town.'

The officer looks at him and the batman walks on to the garden gate, from where he shouts to us again:

'Get out, you! Not stay! Not understand, fools?'

He goes off. The officer smiles at us, then takes us into his room. He sits down on a chair, draws us to him, picks us up and puts us on his knees. We put our arms around his neck, we press ourselves against his hairy chest. He rocks us to and fro.

Beneath us, between the officer's legs, we feel a warm movement. We look at one another, then we look the officer straight in the eyes. He gently pushes us away, ruffles our hair and stands up. He hands us two whips and lies face down on his belly. He says only one word which, without knowing his language, we understand.

We hit him, first one, then the other.

The officer's back is marked with red lines. We hit harder and harder. The officer moans and, without changing position, pulls down his trousers and underpants to his ankles. We hit his white buttocks, his thighs, his legs, his back, his neck, his shoulders as hard as we can and everything becomes red.

The officer's body, hair and clothes, the sheets, the carpets, our hands, our arms are all red. The blood even squirts into our eyes, mingles with our sweat and we go on striking until the man utters a final, inhuman cry and we drop, exhausted, at the foot of his bed.

The Foreign Language

The officer brings us a dictionary in which we can learn his language. We learn the words; the batman corrects our pronunciation. A few weeks later, we speak this new language fluently. We continue to make progress. The batman no longer has to translate. The officer is very pleased with us. He gives us a mouth organ as a present. He also gives us a key to his room so that we can go in there when we like (we already did so with our key, but secretly). Now we no longer need to hide and we can do whatever we like: eat biscuits and chocolate, smoke cigarettes.

We often go into the room, because everything is clean there and it's quieter than in the kitchen. It is there that we usually do our studying.

The officer has a gramophone and records. Lying on the bed, we listen to music. Once, in order to please the officer, we put on his country's national anthem. But he got angry and smashed the record with his fist.

Sometimes we sleep on the bed, which is very wide. One morning, the batman finds us there; he isn't very pleased:

'You very imprudent! You no more do silly thing like that. What happen once, if the officer come back at night?'

'What would happen? There's enough room for him, too.'

The batman says:

'You very stupid. Once you pay your stupidity. If the officer hurt you, I kill him.'

'He won't hurt us. Don't worry about us.'

One night, the officer comes home and finds us asleep on his bed. The light from the oil lamp wakes us. We ask:

'Do you want us to go into the kitchen?'

The officer strokes our heads and says:

'Stay there. Do stay.'

He undresses and lies down between us. He put his arms around us and whispers in our ears:

'Sleep. I love you. Sleep well.'

We go back to sleep. Later, near morning, we want to get up, but the officer holds us back.

'Don't move. Go back to sleep.'

'We want to urinate. We must go.'

'Don't go. Do it here.'

We ask:

'Where?'

He says:

'On me. Yes. Don't be afraid. Piss! On my face.'

We do it, then we go out into the garden, because the bed is all wet. The sun has already risen; we start our morning tasks.

The Officer's Friend

Sometimes the officer comes back with a friend, another, younger officer. They spend the evening together and the friend spends the night. We have observed them several times through the hole in the ceiling.

It's a summer's evening. The batman is making something on the paraffin stove. He puts a cloth on the table and we arrange flowers on it. The officer and his friend are sitting at the table; they are drinking. Later, they eat. The batman eats near the door, sitting on a stool. Then they drink again. Meanwhile, we look after the music. We change the records and wind up the gramophone.

The officer's friend says:

'These kids annoy me. Send them out.'

The officer asks:

'Are you jealous?'

The friend answers:

'Of them? Don't be grotesque! Two little savages like them.'

'They're beautiful, don't you think?'

'Perhaps. I haven't looked at them.'

'Really, you haven't looked at them? Then look at them.'

The friend blushes:

'What do you mean? They annoy me with their cunning ways. As if they were listening to us, spying on us.'

'But they are listening to us. They speak our language perfectly. They understand everything.'

The friend goes pale and gets up:

'This is too much! I'm off!'

The officer says:

'Don't be a fool. Off you go, you kids.'

We leave the room and go up into the attic. We look and listen.

The officer's friend says:

'You made me look ridiculous in front of those stupid kids.'

The officer says:

'They are the two most intelligent children I have ever known.'

The friend says:

'You're just saying that to hurt me. You do everything to torment and humiliate me. One day I'll kill you!'

The officer throws his revolver on the table:

'If only you would. Take it. Kill me! Go on!'

The friend picks up the revolver and points it at the officer:

'I shall do it. You'll see, I shall do it. The next time you speak to me about him, about the other one, I'll kill you.'

The officer shuts his eyes and smiles:

'He was handsome . . . young . . . strong . . . graceful . . . delicate . . . cultivated . . . tender . . . dreamy . . . brave . . . insolent . . . I loved him. He died on the Eastern Front. He was nineteen. I can't live without him.'

The friend throws the revolver on the table and says:

'Swine!'

The officer opens his eyes and looks at his friend:

'What a coward you are! What a spineless character!'

The friend says:

'You have only to do it yourself, if you're so brave . . . and so grief-stricken. If you can't live without him, follow him into death. Or do you need me to help you? I'm not crazy! Die! Die alone!'

The officer picks up the revolver and points it at his temple. We come down from the attic. The batman is sitting in front of the open door of the room. We ask him:

'Do you think he's going to kill himself?'

The batman laughs:

'You, have no fear. They always do that when drink too much. I unload two revolvers before.'

We go into the room and say to the officer:

'We will kill you if you really want us to. Give us your revolver.'

The friend says:

'Little bastards!'

The officer smiles and says:

'Thank you. That's very kind of you, but we were only playing. Go to bed now.'

He gets up to shut the door behind us and sees the batman:

'Are you still there?'

The batman says:

'I haven't been given permission to go.'

'Be off with you! I want to be left in peace! Understand?'

Through the door we can still hear him saying to his friend:

'What a lesson for you, you drip!'

We also hear the noise of a fight, blows, the din of chairs being knocked over, a fall, shouts, panting. Then everything goes quiet.

Our First Show

The housekeeper often sings. Old popular songs and the latest songs about the war. We listen to these songs and practise them on our mouth organ. We also ask the batman to teach us songs of his country.

Late one evening, when Grandmother has already gone to bed, we go into town. Near the castle, in an old street, we stop in front of a single-storey building. Noise, voices and smoke are coming from the door, which opens on to a staircase. We go down the stone steps and find ourselves in a cellar converted into a café. Men, standing or sitting on wooden benches and barrels, are drinking wine. Most of them are old, but there are also a few young ones and three women. No one takes any notice of us.

One of us starts to play on the mouth organ and the other sings a well-known song about a woman waiting for her husband, who has gone to the war and who will come home soon, victorious.

Gradually everybody turns towards us; the voices die down. We sing and play louder and louder, we hear our melody echo in the vaulted ceiling of the cellar, as if it were someone else playing and singing.

When we have finished our song, we look up at the tired, hollow faces. A woman laughs and applauds. A young, one-armed man says in a husky voice:

'More. Play something else!'

We exchange roles. The one who has been playing the mouth organ hands it to the other and we begin a new song.

A very thin man staggers up to us and shouts in our faces:

'Silence, you dogs!'

He pushes us roughly aside, one to the left, one to the right; we lose our balance; the mouth organ drops on to the floor. The man goes up the stairs, holding on to the wall. We can still hear him shouting in the street:

'Be quiet everyone! Be quiet everyone!'

We pick up the mouth organ and clean it. Someone says:

'He's deaf.'

Someone else says:

'He's not only deaf. He's completely mad.'

An old man strokes our hair. Tears are flowing from his deep-sunk, black-encircled eyes.

'What misery! What a miserable world! Poor kids! Poor world!'

A woman says:

'Deaf or mad, at least he came back. You, too, came back.'

She sits down on the knees of the one-armed man, who says:

'You're right, my beauty, I have come back. But what am I going to work with? What am I going to hold the plank to be sawn with? My empty coat-sleeve?'

Another young man, sitting on a bench, says, laughing:

'I, too, have come back. But I'm paralysed from the waist down. The legs and all the rest. I shall never get it up again. I'd rather have gone straight away, in one go, and stayed there.'

Another woman says:

'You're never satisfied. All those I see dying in the hospital say: "Whatever state I'm in, I'd rather survive and go home, see my wife, my mother, and live a little longer.'"

A man says:

'You shut up. Women have seen nothing of the war.'

The woman says:

'Seen nothing? Silly bugger! We've all the work and all the worry: the children to feed and the wounded to look after. Once the war is over, you men are all heroes. The dead: heroes. The survivors: heroes. The maimed: heroes. That's why you men invented war. It's your war. You wanted it, so get on with it. Heroes, my arse!'

Everybody starts talking and shouting. The old man near us says:

'Nobody wanted this war. Nobody. Nobody.'

We leave the cellar and decide to go home.

The streets and the dusty road that lead to Grandmother's are lit by moonlight.

We Extend Our Repertoire

We are learning to juggle with fruit: apples, walnuts, apricots. First with two, that's easy, then with three, four, until we manage five.

We invent conjuring tricks with cards and cigarettes.

We are also training to do acrobatics. We can do cartwheels, somersaults backwards and forwards, and we can walk on our hands with perfect ease.

We dress up in really old clothes that are too big for us and which we found in the attic trunk: loose-fitting, torn checked jackets and wide trousers, which we tie round the waist with string. We have also found a round, hard, black hat.

One of us sticks a red pepper on his nose and the other a false moustache made up of a couple of corn-cob beards. We get hold of some lipstick and extend our mouths to our ears.

Dressed up as clowns, we go out to the market-place. That's where most of the shops are and where most people gather.

We begin our show by making a lot of noise with our mouth organ and with a marrow, which we have hollowed out and turned into a drum. When there are enough spectators around us, we juggle with tomatoes or even with eggs. The tomatoes are real tomatoes, but the eggs have been emptied and filled with fine sand. People don't know this, so they cry out, laugh and applaud when we pretend that we have nearly dropped one.

We continue our show with conjuring tricks and we end it with acrobatics.

While one of us goes on doing cartwheels and somer-saults, the other walks around among the spectators on his hands, holding the old hat between his teeth.

In the evening we do the cafés, wearing our normal clothes.

We soon know all the cafés in the town, the cellars where the proprietor sells his own wine, the drinking places where one drinks standing up, the smarter cafés fre-quented by well-dressed people and a few officers looking for girls to pick up.

People who drink part easily with their money. They confide in people easily, too. We learn all kinds of secrets about all kinds of people.

Often people offer to buy us drinks and, gradually, we are getting used to alcohol. We also smoke the cigarettes that people give us.

We are very successful wherever we go. People think we have good voices, applaud us and call us back several times.

Theatre

Sometimes, if people are attentive, not too drunk and not too noisy, we put on one of our little plays, for example, *The Story of the Poor Man and the Rich Man*.

One of us plays the poor man, the other the rich man.

The rich man is sitting at a table, smoking. Enter the poor man:

'I've finished cutting up your wood, sir.'

'Good. Exercise is very good for you. You look very well. Your cheeks are quite red.'

'My hands are frozen, sir.'

'Come here! Show them to me! It's disgusting! Your hands are all chapped and covered with sores.'

'They're chilblains, sir.'

'You poor people are always getting disgusting illnesses. You're dirty, that's the trouble with you. Here, this is for your work.'

He throws a packet of cigarettes to the poor man, who lights one and starts to smoke it. But there's no ashtray where he is standing near the door and he doesn't dare to go near the table. So he flicks the ash from his cigarette into the palm of his hand. The rich man, who would like the poor man to leave, pretends not to see that the man needs an ashtray. But the poor man doesn't want to leave the premises so quickly because he is hungry. He says:

'There's a good smell in your house, sir.'

'It smells of cleanliness.'

'It also smells of hot soup. I haven't eaten today yet.'

'You should have. Personally, I'm dining out today, in a restaurant, because I've given my cook the day off.'

The poor man sniffs:

'It smells of good hot soup, all the same.'

The rich man shouts:

'It can't smell of soup here; nobody is making soup here; it must be coming from one of the neighbours, or you're just imagining it! You poor people think of nothing but your stomachs; that's why you never have any money; you spend all you have on soup and sausage. You're pigs, that's what you are. And now you're dirtying my floor with your cigarette ash! Get out of here and don't let me see you again!'

The rich man opens the door, kicks out the poor man, who falls flat on his face on the pavement.

The rich man shuts the door, sits down in front of a plate of soup and says, joining his hands:

'I give thanks to Thee, Lord Jesus, for all Thy mercies.'

The Air Raids

When we first came to Grandmother's, there were very few air raids in the Little Town. Now there are more and more of them. The sirens start to wail at any time of the day and night, exactly as in the Big Town. People run into cellars for shelter. Meanwhile, the streets are deserted. Sometimes the doors of houses and shops are left open. We take advantage of this to go in and quietly take whatever we like.

We never shelter in our cellar. Nor does Grandmother. During the day, we carry on with whatever we are doing and at night we carry on sleeping.

Most of the time, the planes only cross over our town and drop their bombs on the other side of the frontier. Sometimes, however, a bomb does drop on a house. In which case, we locate the place from the direction of the smoke and go and see what has been destroyed. If there is anything left to take, we take it.

We have noticed that the people who are in the cellar of a bombed house are always dead. On the other hand, the chimney-stack of the house almost always remains standing.

Sometimes, too, a plane dives in order to machine-gun people in the fields or in the street.

The batman has taught us that we must be very careful when a plane is moving towards us, but that as soon as it is over our heads, the danger has passed.

Because of the air raids, it is forbidden to light lamps

at night unless the windows are completely blacked out. Grandmother thinks it is more practical not to put the lights on at all. Patrols do their rounds all night to make sure the regulation is obeyed.

One day, during a meal, we are talking about a plane we saw fall in flames. We also saw the pilot parachute from it.

'We don't know what happened to him, the enemy pilot.'

Grandmother says:

'Enemy? They are friends, our brothers. They'll be here soon.'

One day, we are out walking during an air raid. A terrified man dashes up to us:

'You mustn't stay out during air raids.'

He pulls us by the arm towards a door:

'Go in, go in there.'

'We don't want to.'

'It's a shelter. You'll be safe there.'

He opens the door and pushes us in front of him. The cellar is full of people. Complete silence reigns there. The women are clutching their children to them.

Suddenly, somewhere, bombs go off. The explosions get nearer. The man who brought us to the cellar runs over to a pile of coal in one corner and tries to bury himself in it.

Some women snigger contemptuously. An elderly woman says:

'His nerves are all upset. He's on leave because of that.'

Suddenly we find it difficult to breathe. We open the cellar door; a big fat woman pushes us back and shuts the door again. She shouts:

'Are you mad? You can't go out now.'

We say:

'People always die in cellars. We want to go out.'

The fat woman leans against the door. She shows us her Civil Protection arm band.

'I'm in charge here! You'll stay here!'

We sink our teeth into her fleshy forearms; we kick her in the shins. She shouts out and tries to hit us. People laugh. In the end, all red with anger and shame, she says:

'Get out! Go and get yourselves killed outside! It'll be no great loss.'

Outside, we can breathe. It's the first time we have been afraid.

The bombs continue to rain down.

The Human Herd

We have come to the presbytery to fetch our clean washing. We are eating bread and butter with the housekeeper in the kitchen. We hear shouting coming from the street. We put down our bread and butter and go out. People are standing in front of their houses; they are looking in the direction of the station. Excited children are running about shouting:

'They're coming! They're coming!'

At the street corner an army Jeep appears with foreign officers. The Jeep is moving slowly forward, followed by soldiers carrying their rifles slung across their shoulders. Behind them is a sort of humen herd. Children like us. Women like our mother. Old men like the cobbler.

Two or three hundred of them pass by, flanked by soldiers. A few women are carrying their young children on their backs, on their shoulders or are pressing them against their breasts. One of them falls; hands stretch out to catch the child and the mother; others carry them, because a soldier has already pointed his rifle at them.

Nobody speaks, nobody cries; their eyes are fixed on the ground. All one can hear is the sound of the soldiers' studded boots.

Just in front of us, a thin arm emerges from the crowd. A dirty hand is held out and a voice asks:

'Bread?'

The housekeeper smiles and pretends to offer the rest of her bread; she holds it closer to the outstretched hand, then, with a great laugh, brings the piece of bread back to her mouth, takes a bite and says:

'I'm hungry, too.'

A soldier who has seen all this gives the housekeeper a great slap on her behind; he pinches her cheek and she waves to him with her handkerchief until all we can see is a cloud of dust against the setting sun.

We go back to the house. From the kitchen we can see the parish priest, kneeling in front of the big crucifix in his room.

The housekeeper says:

'Finish your bread and butter.'

We say:

'We aren't hungry any more.'

We go into the room. The priest turns round:

'Do you want to pray with me, my children?'

'We never pray, as you know very well. We want to understand.'

'You cannot understand. You are too young.'

'*You* are not too young. That's why we are asking *you*. Who are those people? Where are they being taken? Why?'

The priest gets up and comes towards us. Closing his eyes he says:

'The Ways of the Lord are unfathomable.'

He opens his eyes and places his hands on our heads:

'It is unfortunate that you have had to witness such a spectacle. You are trembling all over.'

'So are you, Father.'

'Yes, I am old, I am trembling.'

'And we are cold. We came here stripped to the waist. We are going to put on the shirts that your housekeeper has washed.'

We go into the kitchen. The housekeeper hands us our parcel of clean washing. We each take a shirt. The housekeeper says:

'You're too sensitive. The best thing you can do is to forget what you've seen.'

'We never forget anything.'

She pushes us to the door:

'Off you go and don't worry! None of that has anything to do with you. It'll never happen to you. Those people are only animals.'

Grandmother's Apples

We run from the presbytery to the cobbler's house. His windowpanes have been broken and his door has been smashed in. Inside, everything has been looted. Obscenities have been written over the walls.

An old woman is sitting on a bench in front of the house next door. We ask her:

'Has the cobber gone away?'

'A long time ago, the poor man.'

'Wasn't he among those who went through the town today?'

'No, those who came today came from somewhere else. In cattle trucks. He was killed here, in his workshop, with his own tools. Don't worry. God sees everything. He will recognize His Own.'

When we get home, we find Grandmother lying on her back, her legs apart, in front of the garden gate, apples scattered all around her.

Grandmother doesn't move. Her forehead is bleeding.

We run to the kitchen, wet a cloth and take the brandy down from the shelf. We put the wet cloth on to Grandmother's forehead and pour brandy into her mouth. After a while she opens her eyes and says:

'More!'

We pour more brandy into her mouth.

She sits up and starts shouting:

'Pick up the apples! What are you waiting for, sons of a bitch?'

We pick up the apples lying in the dusty road. We place them in her apron.

The damp cloth has fallen from Grandmother's forehead. Blood is trickling into her eyes. She wipes it away with a corner of her shawl. We ask:

'Are you hurt, Grandmother?'

She sniggers:

'It'll take more than a blow from a rifle butt to kill me off.'

'What happened, Grandmother?'

'Nothing. I was picking apples. I came to the gate to watch the procession. I let go of my apron; the apples fell and rolled on to the road. In the middle of the procession. That was no reason to hit me.'

'Who hit you, Grandmother?'

'Who do you think? You're no fools! They hit them, too. They hit people in the crowd. But there were still some of them who were able to eat my apples!'

We help Grandmother to get up. We take her into the house. She starts peeling the apples to make a compote, but she falls down and we carry her to her bed. We take off her shoes. Her shawl slips off and we see that she is completely bald. We put back her shawl. We stay for a long time at her bedside, holding her hand and observing her breathing.

The Policeman

We are having our breakfast with Grandmother. A man comes into the kitchen without knocking. He shows his police card.

Immediately, Grandmother starts shouting:

'I don't want the police in my house! I've done nothing!'

The policeman says:

'No, nothing, never. Just a few little poisonings here and there.'

Grandmother says:

'Nothing was ever proved. You can't do anything to me.'

The policeman says:

'Take it easy, Grandmother. We're not going to dig up the dead. We've got enough to do burying them.'

'Then what do you want?'

The policeman looks at us and says:

'Chips off the old block, eh?'

Grandmother looks at us, too:

'I hope so. What have you been doing now, sons of a bitch?'

The policeman asks:

'Where were you yesterday evening?'

We answer:

'Here.'

'You weren't hanging around the cafés, as usual?'

'No. We stayed here because Grandmother had an accident.'

Grandmother says very quickly:

'I fell down as I was going down into the cellar. The steps have moss growing on them and I slipped. I banged my head. The kids took me back up and looked after me. They stayed at my bedside all night.'

The policeman says:

'You've got a bad bump there, I can see. You must be careful at your age. Very well. We're going to search the house. Come with me all three of you. We'll start with the cellar.'

Grandmother opens the cellar door and we go down. The policeman moves everything, the sacks, the cans, the baskets and the piles of potatoes.

Grandmother asks us in a whisper:

'What's he looking for?'

We shrug our shoulders.

After the cellar, the policeman searches the kitchen. Then Grandmother has to unlock her room. The policeman searches her bed. There is nothing in the bed, or in the straw mattress, just a bit of cash under the pillow.

In front of the door of the officer's room, the policeman asks:

'What's in here?'

Grandmother says:

'It's a room I let to a foreign officer. I don't have the key.'

The policeman looks at the door to the attic:

'You don't have a ladder?'

Grandmother says:

'It's broken.'

'How do you get up there?'

'I don't go up there. Only the kids go up there.'

The policeman says:

'Well, then, get up there, you kids.'

We climb up into the attic by means of the rope. The policeman opens the chest in which we have arranged everything we need for our studies: Bible, dictionary, paper, pencils and the Big Notebook in which everything is written. But the policeman hasn't come to read. He rummages again through the pile of old clothes and blankets and we go down again. Once down, the policeman looks around him and says:

'I obviously can't dig up the whole garden. Right. Come with me.'

He takes us into the forest, at the side of the big hole where we once found a corpse. The corpse isn't there any more. The policeman asks:

'Have you ever been here before?'

'No. Never. We would have been afraid to go so far.'

'You've never seen this hole, or a dead soldier?'

'No, never.'

'When they found that dead soldier, his rifle, his cartridges and his grenades were missing.'

We say:

'He must have been very absent-minded and careless that soldier, to have lost all those things so indispensable to a soldier.'

The policeman says:

'He didn't lose them. They were stolen from him after he died. You often come into the forest, haven't you any ideas on the matter?'

'No. No ideas.'

'Yet someone certainly took that rifle, those cartridges and those grenades.'

We say:

'Who would dare to touch such dangerous things?'

The Interrogation

We are in the policeman's office. He is sitting at a table and we are standing in front of him. He gets pencil and paper. He is smoking. He asks us questions:

'How long have you known the housekeeper at the presbytery?'

'Since the spring.'

'Where did you meet her?'

'At Grandmother's. She came for potatoes.'

'You deliver wood to the presbytery. How much are you paid for that?'

'Nothing. We take wood to the presbytery in order to thank the housekeeper for doing our washing.'

'Is she nice to you?'

'Very nice. She makes bread and butter for us, cuts our nails and hair and lets us have baths there.'

'Like a mother, in fact. And the parish priest, is he nice to you?'

'Very nice. He lends us books and teaches us a lot of things.'

'When did you last take wood to the presbytery?'

'Five days ago. On Tuesday morning.'

The policeman walks up and down the room. He draws the curtains and turns on his desk lamp. He draws up two chairs and tells us to sit down. He points the lamp at our faces:

'Are you very fond of the housekeeper?'

'Yes, very fond of her.'

'Do you know what has happened to her?'

'Has something happened to her?'

'Yes. Something appalling. This morning, as usual, she was lighting the fire and the kitchen stove blew up. It hit her full in the face. She's in hospital.'

The policeman stops talking; we say nothing. He then says:

'Haven't you anything to say?'

We say:

'If something blows up in your face, you're bound to end up in hospital, or even in the morgue. It's a good thing she isn't dead.'

'She's disfigured for life!'

We say nothing. Nor does the policeman. He looks at us. We look at him. At last he says:

'You don't look particularly sad about it.'

'We're glad she's alive after such an accident.'

'It wasn't an accident. Someone hid an explosive in the firewood. A cartridge from an army rifle. We've found the case.'

We ask:

'Why would anyone do that?'

'To kill her, her or the priest.'

We say:

'People are cruel. They like to kill. It's war that has taught them that. And there are explosives lying around everywhere.'

The policeman starts to shout:

'Stop trying to be clever! You deliver the wood to the presbytery! You hang around all day in the forest! You strip the corpses! You're quite capable of doing anything! You have it in your blood! Your grandmother, too, has a murder on her conscience. She poisoned her husband.

With her it's poison, with you explosives! Admit it, you little bastards! Admit it! It was you, wasn't it?'

We say:

'We aren't the only ones to deliver wood to the presbytery.'

He says:

'That's true. There's also the old man. I've already questioned him.'

We say:

'Anyone can hide a cartridge in a pile of wood.'

'Yes, but not anybody could have cartridges. I'm not interested in your housekeeper! What I want to know is where the cartridges are? And the grenades? And the rifle? The old man has admitted everything. I've questioned him so well that he has admitted everything. But he couldn't show me where the cartridges, the grenades and rifle are. He's not the guilty one. It's you! You know where the cartridges, the grenades and the rifle are and you're going to tell me!'

We say nothing. The policeman hits us – with both hands. Blows from right and left. We are bleeding from the nose and mouth.

'Admit it!'

We say nothing. He goes quite white, he hits us over and over again. We fall off our chairs. He kicks us in the ribs, in the kidneys and in the stomach.

'Admit it! Admit it! It was you! Admit it!'

We can't open our eyes any more. We can't hear anything any more. Our bodies are covered with sweat, blood, urine and excrement. We lose consciousness.

In Prison

We are lying on the hard dirt floor of a cell. Through a tiny barred window, a little light is coming in. But we don't know what time it is, or even if it is morning or afternoon.

Our bodies hurt all over. The slightest movement makes us fall back into semi-consciousness. We can see only indistinctly, there is a buzzing in our ears and a pounding in our heads. We are terribly thirsty. Our mouths are dry.

Hours go by. We don't talk to one another. Later, the policeman comes in and asks us:

'Do you need anything?'

We say:

'Something to drink.'

'Talk. Make a confession. And you'll have as much as you want to eat and drink.'

We say nothing. He asks:

'Grandfather, do you want to eat anything?'

Nobody answers. He goes out.

We realize we aren't alone in the cell. Carefully we raise our heads a little and see an old man lying, huddled up in a corner. Slowly we crawl over towards him and touch him. He is stiff and cold. We crawl back to our place near the door.

It is already night when the policeman comes back with a flash-lamp. He points it at the old man and says:

'Sleep well. Tomorrow morning you can go home.'

He points the lamp straight in our faces, one after the other:

'Still nothing to say? Please yourselves. I can wait. You'll either talk or die here.'

Later in the night the door opens again. The policeman, the batman and the foreign officer come in. The officer bends down and looks at us. He says to the batman:

'Telephone to the base for an ambulance!'

The batman goes out. The officer examines the old man. He says:

'He's beaten him to death!'

He turns to the policeman:

'You'll pay dear for this, you vermin! If you only knew how you'll pay for all this!'

The policeman asks us:

'What did he say?'

'He says that the old man is dead and that you'll pay dear for it, you vermin!'

The officer strokes our foreheads:

'My poor little boys. Did he dare to hurt you, that filthy pig!'

The policeman says:

'What's he going to do to me? Tell him I've got children . . . I didn't know . . . Is he your father, or something?'

We say:

'He's our uncle.'

'You should have told me. I wasn't to know. I'm very sorry. What can I do to . . .'

We say:

'Pray to God.'

The batman arrives with other soldiers. They put us on to stretchers and carry us out to the ambulance. The officer sits beside us. The policeman, flanked by several soldiers, is taken off in the Jeep, driven by the batman.

At the army base, a doctor examines us immediately in

a big, white room. He disinfects our wounds, gives us injections to reduce the pain and against tetanus. He also does X-rays on us. We haven't broken anything, except a few teeth, but they are only milk teeth.

The batman takes us back to Grandmother's. He puts us in the officer's big bed and lies down on a blanket beside the bed. In the morning, he goes to fetch Grandmother, who brings us warm milk in bed.

When the batman has left, Grandmother asks us:

'Did you confess?'

'No, Grandmother. We had nothing to confess.'

'That's what I thought. And what happened to the policeman?'

'We don't know. But he certainly won't come back any more.'

Grandmother sniggers:

'Deported or shot, eh? The pig! We'll celebrate that. I'll go and heat up the chicken I cooked yesterday. I haven't eaten any of it either yet.'

At midday, we get up and go to eat in the kitchen.

During the meal, Grandmother says:

'I wonder why you wanted to kill her? You had your reasons, I suppose.'

The Old Gentleman

Just after the evening meal, an old gentleman arrives with a girl, who is taller than us.

Grandmother asks him:

'What do you want?'

The old gentleman says her name and Grandmother says to us:

'Go out. Go for a walk in the garden.'

We go out. We go round the house and crouch down under the kitchen window. We listen. The old gentleman says:

'Have pity on her.'

Grandmother replies:

'How can you ask me such a thing?'

The old gentleman says:

'You knew her parents. They entrusted her to me before being deported. They gave me your address in case it ever happened that she was no longer safe with me.'

Grandmother asks:

'You know what I'd be risking?'

'Yes, I know, but it's a matter of life and death.'

'There's a foreign officer in the house.'

'Precisely. No one will look for her here. All you'll have to say is that she's your grand-daughter, the cousin of those two boys.'

'Everyone knows I have no other grandchildren except those two boys.'

'You can say she's from your son-in-law's family.'

Grandmother sniggers:

'But I've never seen my son-in-law!'

After a long pause, the old gentleman goes on:

'I'm only asking you to feed the little girl for a few months – till the end of the war.'

'The war may go on for years.'

'No, it won't last much longer now.'

Grandmother starts to snivel:

'I'm just a poor old woman killing herself with work. How can I feed so many mouths?'

The old gentleman says:

'Here's all the money her parents had – and the family jewels. It's all yours if you'll save her.'

Shortly afterwards, Grandmother calls us in:

'This is your cousin.'

We say:

'Yes, Grandmother.'

The old gentleman says:

'You'll play together, the three of you, won't you?'

We say:

'We never play.'

He asks:

'What do you do, then?'

'We work, we study, we do exercises.'

He says:

'I understand. You're serious men. You haven't time to play. You'll look after your cousin, won't you?'

'Yes, sir. We'll look after her.'

'Thank you.'

Our cousin says:

'I'm taller than you.'

We answer:

'But there are two of us.'

The old gentleman says:

'You're right. Two are much stronger than one. And don't forget to call her "cousin", will you?'

'No, sir. We never forget anything.'

'I'm depending on you.'

Our Cousin

Our cousin is five years older than us. Her eyes are dark. Her hair is reddish because of something called henna.

Grandmother tells us that our cousin is the daughter of Father's sister. We say the same thing to those who ask questions about our cousin.

We know that Father has no sister. But we also know that, without that lie, our cousin's life would be in danger – and we've promised the old gentleman to look after her.

When the old gentleman has gone, Grandmother says:

'Your cousin will sleep with you in the kitchen.'

We say:

'There's no more room in the kitchen.'

Grandmother says:

'Sort it out among yourselves.'

Our cousin says:

'I'm quite willing to sleep under the table, on the floor, if you give me a blanket.'

We say:

'You can sleep on the seat and keep the blankets. We'll sleep in the attic. It's not very cold now.'

She says:

'I'll come and sleep in the attic with you.'

'We don't want you. You must never set foot in the attic.'

'Why?'

We say:

'You have a secret. We have one, too. If you don't respect our secret, we won't respect yours.'

She asks:

'Would you be capable of denouncing me?'

'If you go up into the attic, you die. Is that clear?'

She looks at us for a moment in silence, then she says:

'I see. You two little bastards are completely round the bend. I'll never go up into your filthy attic, I promise.'

She keeps her promise and never goes up into the attic. But, everywhere else, she bothers us the whole time.

She says:

'Bring me some raspberries.'

We say:

'Go and get yourself some in the garden.'

She says:

'Stop reading aloud. You're giving me a headache.'

We go on reading.

She asks:

'What are you doing there, lying on the floor, without moving for hours?'

We continue our immobility exercise even when she throws rotten fruit at us.

She says:

'Stop saying nothing, you're getting on my nerves!'

We continue with our silence exercise without answering.

She asks:

'Why aren't you eating anything today?'

'It's our fasting day.'

Our cousin doesn't work, doesn't study, doesn't do exercises. Often she stares at the sky, sometimes she cries.

Grandmother never hits our cousin. She never swears at her. She doesn't ask her to work. She doesn't ask her to do anything. She never speaks to her.

Jewels

The same evening our cousin arrives, we go and sleep in the attic. We take two blankets from the officer's room and lay hay on the floor. Before going to bed, we look through the holes. In the officer's room there is nobody. In Grandmother's room there is a light on, which doesn't happen very often.

Grandmother has taken the oil lamp from the kitchen and has hung it over her dressing table. This is an old piece of furniture with three mirrors. The one in the middle is fixed, the other two move. You can move them to see yourself in profile.

Grandmother is sitting in front of the dressing table, looking at herself in the mirror. On her head, over her black shawl, she has placed something shiny. Around her neck hang several necklaces, her arms are covered with bracelets, her fingers with rings. She is talking to herself as she contemplates her reflection:

'Rich, rich. It's easy to be beautiful with all that. Easy. The wheel turns. They're mine, now, the jewels. Mine. It's only fair. How they shine! How they shine!'

Later, she says:

'And what if they come back? What if they ask for them back? Once the danger is over, they forget. They don't know what gratitude is. They promise the earth and then . . . No, no, they're already dead. The old gentleman will die, too. He said I could keep everything . . . But the girl . . . She saw everything, heard everything, she'll want to get them back, that's for sure. After the war, she'll claim them back. But I don't want to give them back – I cannot. They're mine. For ever . . . She must die, too. Then there'll be no proof. No one'll be any the wiser. Yes, the girl will have to die. She'll have an accident. Just before the end of the war. Yes, it will have to be an accident. Not poison. Not this time. An accident. Drowned in the stream. Hold her head under the water. Difficult. Push her down the cellar steps. Not high enough. Poison. There's only poison. Something slow. Small doses. An illness that eats away slowly, for months. There's no doctor. A lot of people die like that, for lack of care, in wartime.'

Grandmother raises her fist and threatens her image in the mirror:

'You can do nothing! Nothing!'

She sniggers. She takes off the jewellery, puts it in a canvas bag and stuffs the bag into her straw mattress. She then goes to bed – and we do, too.

Next morning, when our cousin has gone out of the kitchen, we say to Grandmother:

'Grandmother, we've something to say to you.'

'What now?'

'Listen, Grandmother. We promised the old gentleman to look after our cousin. So nothing must happen to her – either through accident or illness. Nothing. Or to us either.'

We show her a sealed envelope:

'Everything is written down. We are going to give this letter to the priest. If anything happens to any of the three of us, the priest will open the letter. Do you understand, Grandmother?'

Grandmother looks at us, her eyes almost shut. She is breathing very heavily. She says very quietly:

'Sons of a bitch, a whore and the devil! Cursed be the day that you were born.'

In the afternoon, when Grandmother goes off to work in her vineyard, we search her mattress. There is nothing there.

Our Cousin and Her Lover

Our cousin is getting more serious. She doesn't bother us any more. Every day she washes in the big tub that we bought with the money we have earned in the cafés. She washes her dress very often and her knickers, too. While her clothes are drying, she wraps herself in a towel or lies in the sun with her knickers drying on top of her. She is very brown. Her hair covers her to her buttocks. Sometimes she turns on to her back and hides her breasts with her hair.

Towards evening, she goes off to the town. She stays longer and longer in town. One evening, we follow her, without her knowing.

Near the graveyard, she joins a group of boys and girls, all much older than us. They are sitting under the trees, smoking. They've also got bottles of wine. They drink straight from the bottle. One of them keeps watch, sitting on a seat at the edge of the path. If someone comes, he whistles a well-known tune and stays where he is. The group disperses and hides in the bushes or behind the gravestones. When the danger is over, the one keeping watch whistles a different tune.

The group talks very quietly about the war and about desertions, deportations, resistance and liberation.

According to them, the foreign soldiers who are in our country and who claim to be our allies are in fact our enemies and those who will be here soon and win the war are not enemies but, on the contrary, our liberators.

They say:

'My father has gone over to the other side. He'll come back with them.'

'My father deserted when war was declared.'

'My parents joined the partisans. I was too young to go with them.'

'Mine were taken off by those bastards. Deported.'

'You'll never see them again, your parents. Nor will I. They're all dead now.'

'You can't be sure. There'll be survivors.'

'And we'll avenge the dead.'

'We were too young. Pity. We couldn't do anything.'

'It'll be over soon. "They" will be here any day now.'

'We'll be waiting for them in the Town Square with flowers.'

Well into the night, the group disperses. Everybody goes home.

Our cousin goes off with a boy. We follow her. They go into the little lanes around the castle and disappear behind a ruined wall. We can't see them, but we can hear them.

Our cousin says:

'Lie down on me. Yes, like that. Kiss me. Kiss me.'

The boy says:

'You're really beautiful! I want you.'

'Me too. But I'm afraid. What if I get pregnant?'

'I'll marry you. I love you. We'll get married after the Liberation.'

'We're too young. We must wait.'

'I can't wait.'

'Stop! You're hurting me. You mustn't, darling, you mustn't.'

The boy says:

'Yes, you're right. But stroke me. Give me your hand.

Stroke me there, like that. Turn round. I want to kiss you there, there, while you stroke me.'

Our cousin says:

'No, don't do that. I'm ashamed. Oh! Go on, go on! I love you, I love you so much.'

We go home.

The Blessing

We have to go to the presbytery to take back the books we've borrowed.

The door is opened by an old woman again. She lets us in and says:

'The Father is expecting you.'

The priest says:

'Sit down.'

We put the books on his desk. We sit down. The priest looks at us for a moment, then says:

'I was expecting you. You haven't been for a long time.'

We say:

'We wanted to finish the books. And we've been very busy.'

'And what about your bath?'

'We have all we need to wash at home now. We bought a tub, soap, scissors and toothbrushes.'

'What with? Where did you get the money?'

'With the money we earn playing music in the cafés.'

'The cafés are places of perdition. Especially at your age.'

We don't answer. He says:

'You haven't been for the blind old woman's money either. It has amounted to quite a considerable sum now. Take it.'

He hands us the money. We say:

'Keep it. You have given enough. We took your money when it was absolutely necessary. Now we earn enough money to give some to Harelip. We've also taught her to work. We have helped her dig her garden and plant potatoes, beans, marrows and tomatoes. We've given her chicks and rabbits to rear. She looks after her garden and her animals. She doesn't beg any more. She doesn't need your money any more.'

The priest says:

'Then take this money for yourselves. Then you won't have to work in the cafés.'

'We like working in the cafés.'

He says:

'I heard you were beaten and tortured.'

We ask:

'What happened to your housekeeper?'

'She went to the front to look after the wounded. She died.'

We say nothing. He asks:

'Would you like to confide in me? I am sworn to keep the secrets of the confessional. You have nothing to fear. You can confess.'

We say:

'We have nothing to confess.'

'You're wrong. Such a crime is very hard to bear. Confession will make it easier for you. God forgives all those who are sincerely sorry for their sins.'

We say:

'We're sorry for nothing. We have nothing to be sorry about.'

After a long pause he says:

'I saw it all through the window. The piece of bread . . . But vengeance belongs only to God. You have no right to do His work for Him.'

We say nothing. He asks:

'Can I bless you?'

'If you want to.'

He places his hands on our heads:

'Almighty God, bless these thy children. Whatever their crime, forgive them. Poor lambs who have lost their way in an abominable world, themselves victims of our perverted times, they know not what they do. I beg Thee to save their child's souls, to purify them in thy infinite goodness and mercy. Amen.'

Then he says to us again:

'Come back and see me from time to time, even if you don't need anything.'

Flight

From one day to the next, posters appear on the walls of the town. One poster shows an old man lying on the ground, his body pierced by the bayonet of an enemy soldier. Another shows an enemy soldier striking a child with another child, whom he is holding by the feet. Yet another shows an enemy soldier pulling at a woman's arm and, with his other hand, tearing off her bodice. The woman's mouth is open and tears are flowing from her eyes.

The people who look at the posters are terrified.

Grandmother laughs and says:

'It's all lies. You mustn't be afraid.'

People are saying that the Big Town has fallen.

Grandmother says:

'If they've crossed the Big River, nothing will stop them. They'll be here soon.'

Our cousin says:

'Then I'll be able to go home.'

One day, people say that the army has surrendered, there is an armistice and the war is over. Next day, people say that there is a new government and the war is going on.

A lot of foreign soldiers arrive by train or in trucks. There are soldiers from our country, too. There are a lot of wounded. When people ask the soldiers from our country questions, they reply that they don't know anything. They cross the town. They go into the other country through the road that passes by the camp.

People say:

'They're running away. The country has collapsed.'

Others say:

'They're withdrawing and regrouping behind the frontier. They'll stop them here. They'll never let the enemy cross the frontier.'

Grandmother says:

'We'll see.'

Many people pass in front of Grandmother's house. They, too, are going into the other country. They say they are leaving our country for ever, because the enemy is arriving and will take its revenge. It will reduce our people to slavery.

There are people who flee on foot, with bags on their backs, others push their bicycles laden with various objects: a duvet, a violin, a piglet in a cage, saucepans. Others are perched on carts drawn by horses: they are taking all their furniture with them.

Most of them are from our town, but some have come from further away.

One morning, the batman and the foreign officer come to say goodbye.

The batman says:

'It's all over. But it's better to be beaten than dead.'

He laughs. The officer puts a record on the gramophone. We listen to it in silence, sitting on the big bed. The officer holds us tightly in his arms and cries.

'I won't see you any more.'

We say:

'You'll have children of your own.'

'I don't want any.'

He then says, pointing to the records and the gramophone: 'Keep these to remember me by. But not the dictionary. You'll have to learn another language.'

The Charnel-House

One night, we hear explosions, rifle fire and machine-gun fire. We go outside to see what is happening. A big fire is raging on the campsite. We think the enemy has arrived but, next day, the town is silent; all we can hear is the distant rumble of cannon.

At the end of the road leading to the base, there is no sentry any more. Thick, sickly smelling smoke rises up into the sky. We decide to go and see.

We enter the camp. It is empty. There is nobody there. Some of the buildings are still burning. The stench is unbearable, but we hold our noses and keep going. We come up against a barbed-wire fence. We go up a watchtower. We see a big square on which there are four tall, black piles. We spot an opening, a gap in the fence. We go down the watchtower and find the way in. It's a big iron gate, which has been left open. Above it is written in the foreign language: 'Transit Camp'. We go in.

The black piles we saw from above consist of burnt bodies. Some of them have been thoroughly burnt and only the bones remain. Others are scarcely blackened at all. There are many of these. Large and small. Adults and children. We think that they killed them first, then piled them up, poured petrol over them and set light to them.

We vomit. We run out of the camp. We go home. Grandmother calls us in to eat, but we vomit again.

Grandmother says:

'You've been eating some rubbish again.'

We say:

'Yes, green apples.'

Our cousin says:

'The camp has been burnt down. We ought to go and see it. There can't be anybody left there.'

'We've already been. There's nothing of interest.'

Grandmother sniggers:

'Haven't the heroes left anything? They took everything with them? They didn't leave anything useful at all? Did you have a good look?'

'Yes, Grandmother. We had a good look. There's nothing there.'

Our cousin goes out of the kitchen. We follow her. We ask her:

'Where are you going?'

'To town.'

'Already? You usually only go in the evenings.'

She smiles:

'Yes, but I'm expecting someone. That's enough questions now!'

Our cousin smiles at us again, then runs off to the town.

Our Mother

We are in the garden. An army Jeep stops in front of the house. Our mother gets out, followed by a foreign officer. They run across the garden to us. Mother is holding a baby in her arms. She sees us and calls:

'Come along! Get into the Jeep quickly. We're going. Hurry up. Leave everything and come!'

We ask:

'Who's is the baby?'

She says:

'It's your little sister. Come on! There's no time to waste.'

We ask:

'Where are we going?'

'To the other country. Stop asking questions and come along.'

We say:

'We don't want to go there. We want to stay here.'

Mother says:

'I have to go there. And you're coming with me.'

'No. We're staying here.'

Grandmother comes out of the house. She says to Mother:

'What are you doing? What have you got there in your arms?'

Mother says:

'I've come for my sons. I'll send you money, Mother.'

Grandmother says:

'I don't want your money. And I won't give you the boys back.'

Mother asks the officer to take us by force. We quickly climb up into the attic by the rope. The officer tries to catch us, but we kick him in the face. The officer swears. We pull up the rope.

Grandmother sniggers:

'You see, they don't want to go with you.'

Mother shouts at us:

'I order you to come down immediately!'

Grandmother says:

'They never obey orders.'

Mother starts to cry:

'Come along, my darlings. I can't leave without you.'

Grandmother says:

'Your foreign bastard isn't enough?'

We say:

'We like it here, Mother. You go. We're quite happy at Grandmother's.'

We hear cannon and machine-gun fire. The officer puts his arm around Mother's shoulders and guides her towards the car. But Mother slips away:

'They're my sons, I want them! I love them!'

Grandmother says:

'I need them. I'm old. You can have others – as we can see!'

Mother says:

'I beg you, don't keep them.'

Grandmother says:

'I'm not keeping them. Hey, you boys, come down at once and go off with your mother.'

We say:

'We don't want to go. We want to stay with you, Grandmother.'

The officer takes Mother in his arms, but she pushes

him away. The officer goes and sits in the Jeep and starts the engine. At precisely that moment, there is an explosion in the garden. Immediately afterwards, we see Mother on the ground. The officer runs towards her. Grandmother tries to hold us back. She says:

'Don't look! Go back into the house!'

The officer swears, runs to his Jeep and drives off at top speed.

We look at Mother. Her guts are coming out of her belly. She is red all over. So is the baby. Mother's head is hanging in the hole made by the shell. Her eyes are open and still wet with tears.

Grandmother says:

'Go and fetch the spade!'

We lay a blanket at the bottom of the hole and lay Mother on it. The baby is still held to her breast. We cover them with another blanket, then fill in the hole.

Our cousin comes back from town and asks:

'Has anything happened?'

We say:

'Yes, a shell made a hole in the garden.'

Our Cousin Leaves

All night we hear gunfire and explosions. At dawn, everything suddenly goes quiet. We are sleeping in the officer's big bed. His bed has become our bed and his room our room.

In the morning we go and have our breakfast in the kitchen. Grandmother is standing in front of the stove. Our cousin is folding her blankets.

She says:

'I really slept badly last night.'

We say:

'You'll sleep in the garden. There's no more noise and it's warm.'

She asks:

'Weren't you afraid last night?'

We shrug our shoulders and say nothing.

There is a knock at the door. A man in civilian clothes enters, followed by two soldiers. The soldiers are carrying machine-guns and are wearing a uniform we have never seen before.

Grandmother says something in the language she speaks when she drinks her brandy. The soldiers answer. Grandmother flings her arms around their necks and kisses them in turn. Then she goes on talking to them.

The civilian says:

'You speak their language, madam?'

Grandmother replies:

'It's my mother tongue, sir.'

Our cousin asks:

'Are they here? When did they arrive? We wanted to welcome them with bunches of flowers on the Town Square.'

The civilian asks:

'Who's we?'

'My friends and I.'

The civilian smiles:

'Well, it's too late. They arrived last night. And I came just after them. I'm looking for a girl.'

He says a name; our cousin says:

'Yes, that's me. Where are my parents?'

The civilian says:

'I don't know. My job is just to find the children on my list. We'll first go to a reception centre in the Big Town. Then we'll try and find your parents.'

Our cousin says:

'I have a friend here. Is he on your list, too?'

She says the name of her lover. The civilian consults his list:

'Yes. He's already at army headquarters. You'll travel together. Get your things ready.'

Our cousin is very happy. She packs her dresses and gathers all her toiletries together on her bath towel.

The civilian turns to us:

'And what about you? What are your names?'

Grandmother says:

'They're my grandsons. They'll stay with me.'

We say:

'Yes, we'll stay with Grandmother.'

The civilian says:

'I'd like to have your names all the same.'

We tell him them. He looks at his papers.

'You're not on my list. You can keep them, madam.'

Grandmother says:

'What do you mean, I can keep them? Of course I can keep them!'

Our cousin says:

'I'm ready. Let's go.'

The civilian says:

'You're in a great hurry. You might at least thank this lady and say goodbye to these little boys.'

Our cousin says:

'Little boys? Little bastards, you mean.'

She gives us a big hug.

'I won't kiss you, I know you don't like that. Don't do too many silly things. Take care.'

She gives us an even bigger hug and starts crying. The civilian takes her by the arm and says to Grandmother:

'I would like to thank you, madam, for everything you have done for this child.'

We all go out together. In front of the garden gate, there is a Jeep. The two soldiers sit in front, the civilian and our cousin in the back. Grandmother shouts something. The soldiers laugh. The Jeep moves off. Our cousin doesn't look back.

The Arrival of the New Foreigners

After our cousin has left, we go into town to see what has happened.

There is a tank at every street corner. On the Town Square, there are trucks, Jeeps, motorcycles, side-cars and, everywhere, lots of soldiers. In the market square, which is not asphalted, they are setting up tents and open-air kitchens.

When we go by, they smile at us, talk to us, but we can't understand what they're saying.

Apart from the soldiers, there is nobody in the streets. The doors of the houses are shut, the shutters closed, the shop blinds lowered.

We go home and say to Grandmother:

'Everything is quiet in town.'

She sniggers:

'They're resting for the moment, but this afternoon, you'll see!'

'What is going to happen, Grandmother?'

'They'll carry out searches. They'll go into everybody's house and search it. And they'll take whatever they like. I've lived through one war already and I know what happens. We've nothing to be afraid of: there's nothing to take here and I know how to talk to them.'

'But what are they looking for, Grandmother?'

'Spies, weapons, munitions, watches, gold, women.'

And, in the afternoon, the soldiers do start a systematic search of the houses. If there is no answer, they fire a shot in the air, then batter down the door.

A lot of houses are empty. The residents have left for good or are hiding in the forest. These uninhabited houses are searched like all the others, as well as the shops.

After the soldiers have gone, thieves go into the abandoned shops and houses. The thieves are mainly children and old men, and a few women, too, who are afraid of nothing and are poor.

We meet Harelip. Her arms are full of clothes and shoes. She says to us:

'Hurry up while there is still something left. This is the third time I've done my shopping.'

We go into Booksellers and Stationers – the door has been smashed in. There are only a few children, younger than us. They are taking pencils and coloured chalks, rubbers, pencil sharpeners and schoolbags.

We take our time choosing what we need: a complete encyclopaedia in several volumes, pencils and paper.

In the street, an old man and an old woman are fighting over a smoked ham. They are surrounded by people, urging them on and laughing. The woman scratches the old man's face and, in the end, she goes off with the ham.

The thieves are getting drunk on stolen alcohol, fighting one another, smashing the windows of the houses and shops they have looted, breaking crockery, flinging to the floor whatever they don't need or can't take off with them.

The soldiers are also drinking and are going back to the houses but, this time, to find women.

Everywhere we can hear gunfire and the cries of women being raped.

On the town square, a soldier is playing the accordion. Other soldiers are dancing and singing.

The Fire

For several days now we haven't seen our neighbour in her garden. Nor have we met Harelip. We go and see what has happened.

The door of the house is open. We go in. The windows are small. It is dark in the room, even though the sun is shining outside.

When our eyes have got used to the darkness, we can make out our neighbour, lying on the kitchen table. Her legs are hanging loose, her arms are placed over her face. She doesn't move.

Harelip is lying on the bed. She is naked. Between her spread legs there is a dried pool of blood and sperm. Her eyelashes are stuck together for ever and her lips are curled up over her black teeth in an eternal smile: Harelip is dead.

Our neighbour says:

'Go away.'

We go up to her and ask her:

'You aren't deaf?'

'No. And I'm not blind either. Go away.'

We say:

'We want to help you.'

She says:

'I don't need help. I don't need anything. Go away.'

We ask:

'What happened here?'

'You can see for yourself. She's dead, isn't she?'

'Yes. It was the new foreigners?'

'Yes. She called them in. She went out on to the road and made a sign to them to come. There were twelve or fifteen of them. And as they had her, one after another, she kept shouting: "Oh, this is good, this is good! Come, all of you, come, another one, another one!" She died happy, fucked to death. But I'm not dead! I don't know how long I've been lying here, without eating or drinking. And death still hasn't come. It never does come when you call it. It enjoys torturing us. I've been calling it for years and it pays no attention.'

We ask:

'Do you really want to die?'

'What else could I want? If you want to do something for me, set light to the house. I don't want them to find us like this.'

We say:

'But it'll hurt terribly.'

'Don't bother yourselves about that. Set light to the house, that's all, if you're capable of it.'

'Yes, madam, we are capable of it. You can depend on us.'

We slit her throat with the razor, then we go and siphon off petrol from an army vehicle. We pour the petrol over both bodies and over the walls of the house. We set light to it and go home.

In the morning, Grandmother says:

'The neighbour's house has burnt down. They were both inside, her daughter and her. The girl must have left something on the fire, crazy thing that she is.'

We go back to take the hens and the rabbits, but other neighbours have already taken them during the night.

The End of the War

For weeks now, we have seen the victorious army of the new foreigners, which we now call the army of the Liberators, march past Grandmother's house.

Tanks, cannons, armoured cars and trucks cross the frontier night and day. The front is moving further and further into the neighbouring country.

In the opposite direction comes another procession: the prisoners of war, the defeated. Among them are many men from our own country. They are still wearing their uniforms, but they have been stripped of their weapons – and of their ranks. They march, heads down, to the station, where they are taken off on trains. Nobody knows where they are going to or how long they will be there.

Grandmother says they are being taken far away, to a cold, uninhabited country, where they will be forced to work so hard that none of them will come back. They will all die of cold, exhaustion, hunger and all kinds of diseases.

A month after our country was liberated, it is the end of the war everywhere and the Liberators move into our country, for good, people say. So we ask Grandmother to teach us their language. She says:

'How can I teach it to you? I'm not a teacher.'

We say:

'It's simple, Grandmother. All you have to do is to talk to us in that language all day and, in the end, we'll understand.'

Soon we know enough to act as interpreters between the

local inhabitants and the Liberators. We take advantage of the fact to trade in articles that the army has plenty of, like cigarettes, tobacco and chocolate, which we exchange for what the civilians have – wine, brandy and fruit.

Money has no value any more; everyone barters.

The girls sleep with the soldiers in exchange for silk stockings, jewellery, perfume, watches and other articles that the soldiers have picked up in the towns on their way.

Grandmother doesn't go to the market with her wheelbarrow any more. Instead, well-dressed ladies come to Grandmother's and beg her to exchange a chicken or a sausage for a ring or a pair of earrings.

Ration tickets are distributed. People start queueing in front of the butcher's and baker's as early as four in the morning. The other shops stay shut, because they have nothing to sell.

Everybody is short of everything.

We and Grandmother have everything we need.

Later, we have our own army and government again, but our army and government are controlled by our Liberators. Their flag flies over all the public buildings. The photograph of their leader is displayed everywhere. They teach us their songs and their dances; they show us their films in our cinemas. In the schools, the language of our Liberators is compulsory; other foreign languages are forbidden.

It is forbidden to criticise or make jokes about our Liberators or our new government. You have only to be denounced and you'll be thrown into prison, without trial, whoever you are. Men and women disappear without anyone knowing why and their families will never have news of them.

The frontier has been rebuilt. It cannot now be crossed.
Our country is surrounded by barbed wire; we are completely cut off from the rest of the world.

School Reopens

In autumn, all the children go back to school, except us.
We say to Grandmother:

'Grandmother, we don't want to go to school any more.'

She says:

'I hope not. I need you here. And what more could you learn at school anyway?'

'Nothing, Grandmother, absolutely nothing.'

Soon we receive a letter. Grandmother asks:

'What does it say?'

'It says that you are responsible for us and that we must report to the school.'

Grandmother says:

'Burn the letter. I can't read and you can't either. No one ever read that letter.'

We burn the letter. Soon we get a second. It says that if we don't go to school, Grandmother will be punished by law. We burn that letter, too. We say to Grandmother:

'Grandmother, don't forget that one of us is blind and the other deaf.'

A few days later, a man turns up at our house. He says:

'I'm the inspector of primary schools. You have in your house two children of compulsory school age. You have already received two warnings about this.'

Grandmother says:

'You mean letters? I can't read. Nor can the children.'

One of us asks:

'Who is it? What's he saying?'

The other one says:

'He is asking if we can read. What's he like?'

'He's tall and looks mean.'

We shout out together:

'Go away! Don't hurt us! Don't kill us! Help!'

We hide under the table. The inspector asks Grandmother:

'What's the matter with them? What's wrong with them?'

Grandmother says:

'Oh! The poor things are afraid of everybody! They have lived through such terrible things in the Big Town. What's more, one of them is deaf and the other blind. The deaf one has to explain to the blind one what he can see and the blind one has to explain to the deaf one what he can hear. Otherwise, they don't understand anything.'

Under the table, we yell:

'Help, help! It's blowing up! I can't stand the noise! It's blinding my eyes!'

Grandmother explains:

'When someone frightens them, they hear and see things that aren't there.'

The inspector says:

'They have hallucinations. They should be treated in a hospital.'

We shout even louder.

Grandmother says:

'Nothing could be worse! It was in a hospital it all happened. They were visiting their mother who worked there. When bombs fell on the hospital, they were there, they saw the wounded and the dead; they themselves remained in a coma for several days.'

The inspector says:

'Poor kids. Where are their parents?'

'Dead or disappeared. Who knows?'

'They must be a very heavy burden for you.'

'What can you do? I'm all they have in the world.'

Before leaving, the inspector shakes Grandmother's hand:

'You're a very good woman.'

We receive a third letter in which it says that we have been exempted from attending school on account of our infirmity and our physical trauma.

Grandmother Sells Her Vineyard

An officer comes to see Grandmother. He wants her to sell her vineyard. The army wants to put up a building on her land for the frontier guards.

Grandmother asks:

'And what will you pay me with? Money is worth nothing.'

The officer says:

'In exchange for your land, we'll install running water and electricity in your house.'

Grandmother says:

'I don't need your electricity or your running water. I've always lived without.'

The officer says:

'We could also take your vineyard without giving you anything in exchange. And that's what we're going to do if you don't accept our offer. The army needs your land. Your patriotic duty is to give it to us.'

Grandmother opens her mouth to speak, but we intervene:

'Grandmother, you are old and tired. The vineyard gives you a lot of work and hardly brings anything in. On the other hand, the value of your house will increase a great deal with water and electricity.'

The officer says:

'Your grandsons are more intelligent than you, Grandmother.'

Grandmother says:

'You can say that again! So talk it over with them. Let them decide.'

The officer says:

'But I need your signature.'

'I'll sign whatever you like. Anyway, I can't write.'

Grandmother starts to cry, gets up and says to us:

'I'll leave it to you.'

She goes off to her vineyard.

The officer says:

'She's fond of her vineyard, the poor old woman, isn't she? It's a deal, then?'

We say:

'As you yourself have observed, that land has great sentimental value for her and the army would certainly not want to rob of her hard-earned property a poor old lady who, what's more, is a native of the country of our heroic Liberators.'

The officer says:

'Ah, yes? She's a native . . .'

'Yes. She speaks their language perfectly. And we do, too. And if you have any intention of committing an abuse . . .'

The officer says very quickly:

'No, no! What do you want?'

'In addition to the water and electricity, we want a bathroom.'

'Anything else? And where do you want your bathroom?'

We take him into our room and show him where we want our bathroom.

'Here, leading off our room. Seven to eight square metres. Built-in bath, wash basin, shower, water heater, WC.'

He looks at us for a long time, then says:

'It can be done.'

We say:

'We'd also like a wireless set. We don't have one and it's impossible to buy one.'

He asks:

'And is that all?'

'Yes, that is all.'

He bursts out laughing:

'You'll have your bathroom and your wireless. But I'd have been better off talking to your grandmother.'

Grandmother's Illness

One morning, Grandmother doesn't come out of her room. We knock on her door, call her, but she doesn't answer.

We go to the back of the house and break a windowpane in order to get into her room.

Grandmother is lying in her bed. She isn't moving. Nevertheless she is breathing and her heart is beating. One of us stays with her, the other fetches a doctor.

The doctor examines Grandmother. He says:

'Your grandmother has had an attack of apoplexy, a cerebral haemorrhage.'

'Is she going to die?'

'You can't tell. She's old, but her heart is sound. Give her these medicines, three times a day. And there'll have to be someone to look after her.'

We say:

'We'll look after her. What has to be done?'

'Feed her, wash her. She'll probably be permanently paralysed.'

The doctor leaves. We make a purée of vegetables and feed Grandmother with a small spoon. By evening, it smells very bad in her room. We lift her blankets: her straw mattress is full of excrement.

We fetch straw from a peasant and buy babies' rubber knickers and nappies.

We undress Grandmother, wash her in our bath-tub and make her a clean bed. She is so thin that the babies' knickers fit her very well. We change her nappies several times a day.

A week later, Grandmother begins to move her hand. One morning, she starts swearing at us:

'Sons of a bitch! Go and roast a fowl! How do you expect me to get my strength back with your green vegetable purées? I want some goat's milk, too! I hope you haven't neglected anything while I've been ill?'

'No, Grandmother, we haven't neglected anything.'

'Help me to get up, you good-for-nothings!'

'Grandmother, you must stay in bed, the doctor said so.'

'The doctor, the doctor! That fool! Permanently paralysed, indeed! I'll show him how paralysed I am!'

We help her to get up, accompany her into the kitchen and sit her down on the seat. When the fowl is cooked, she eats it all herself. After the meal, she says:

'What are you waiting for? Make me a good stout stick, hurry up, you lazy-bones, I want to go and see if everything is in order.'

We run off to the forest, find a suitable branch, run back home and, with Grandmother looking on, shape the stick to her size. Grandmother grabs it and threatens us:

'Woe betide you if everything isn't in order!'

She goes out into the garden. We follow her at a distance. She then goes into the privy and we hear her muttering:

'Knickers! What an idea! They're completely mad!'

When she comes back to the house we go and look in the privy. She has thrown the knickers and nappies into the hole.

Grandmother's Treasure

One evening, Grandmother says:

'Shut all the doors and windows. I want to talk to you and I don't want anyone to hear us.'

'Nobody comes this way any more, Grandmother.'

'The frontier guards are always prowling about, as you know. And they're quite capable of listening at people's doors. And bring me a sheet of paper and a pencil.'

We ask:

'You want to write something, Grandmother?'

She shouts:

'Do as your're told! Don't ask questions!'

We shut the windows and doors and bring her the pencil and paper. Grandmother, sitting at the other end of the table, draws something on the sheet of paper. She whispers:

'This is where my treasure is hidden.'

She hands us the sheet of paper. On it she has drawn a rectangle, a cross and, under the cross, a circle. Grandmother asks:

'Do you understand?'

'Yes, Grandmother, we understand. But we knew already.'

'What! What did you know already?'

We reply in a whisper:

'That your treasure was to be found under the cross on Grandfather's grave.'

Grandmother says nothing for a while, then she says:

'I might have known. Have you known for long?'

'For a very long time, Grandmother. Ever since we saw you tending Grandfather's grave.'

Grandmother breathes very heavily:

'There's no point in getting excited. Anyway, it's all yours. You're clever enough now to know what to do with it.'

We say:

'For the moment, there's not much we can do with it.'

Grandmother says:

'No. You're right. You must wait. Will you be able to wait?'

'Yes, Grandmother.'

No one says anything for some time, then Grandmother says:

'That isn't all. When I have a new attack, I want you to know that I don't want your bath, your knickers, or your nappies.'

She gets up and rummages around on the shelf among her bottles. She comes back with a small blue bottle:

'Instead of all your filthy medicines, you'll pour the contents of this bottle into my first cup of milk.'

We say nothing. She shouts:

'Do you understand, sons of a bitch?'

We say nothing. She says:

'Maybe you're afraid of the autopsy, you little brats? There won't be an autopsy. Nobody's going to make a fuss when an old woman dies after a second attack.'

We say:

'We aren't afraid of the autopsy, Grandmother. We just think that you may recover a second time.'

'No. I shan't recover. I know. So we must put an end to it as soon as possible.'

We say nothing and Grandmother starts to cry:

'You don't know what it's like to be paralysed. To see everything, hear everything and not be able to move. If you aren't even capable of doing this simple little thing for me, then you're ungrateful brats, vipers I have nursed in my bosom.'

We say:

'Don't cry, Grandmother. We'll do it; if you really want us to, we'll do it.'

Our Father

When Father arrives, we are all three working in the kitchen, because it's raining outside.

Father stops in front of the door, arms folded, legs apart. He asks:

'Where's my wife?'

Grandmother sniggers:

'Well, well! So she really did have a husband?'

Father says:

'Yes, I'm your daughter's husband. And these are my sons.'

He looks at us and adds:

'You really have grown up. But you haven't changed.'

Grandmother says:

'My daughter, your wife, entrusted the children to me.'

Father says:

'She'd have done better to entrust them to someone else. Where is she? I've been told she went abroad. Is that true?'

Grandmother says:

'That's old, all that. Where have you been until now?'

Father says:

'I've been a prisoner of war. And now I want to find my wife again. Don't try to hide anything from me, you old Witch.'

Grandmother says:

'I really appreciate your way of thanking me for what I've done for your children.'

Father shouts:

'I don't give a damn! Where's my wife?'

Grandmother says:

'You don't give a damn? About your children and me? Well, I'll show you where your wife is!'

Grandmother goes out into the garden and we follow her. With her stick, she points to the flower-bed that we have planted over Mother's grave:

'There! That's where your wife is. In the ground.'

Father asks:

'Dead? From what? When?'

Grandmother says:

'Dead. From a shell. A few days before the end of the war.'

Father says:

'It's forbidden to bury people just anywhere.'

Grandmother says:

'We buried her where she died. And that isn't anywhere. It's my garden. It was also her garden when she was a little girl.'

Father looks at the damp flowers and says:

'I want to see her.'

Grandmother says:

'You shouldn't. We shouldn't disturb the dead.'

Father says:

'In any case, she'll have to be buried in a cemetery. It's the law. Get me a spade.'

Grandmother shrugs her shoulders:

'Get him a spade.'

In the rain, we watch Father demolish our little flower garden and watch him dig. He gets to the blankets and pulls them away. A big skeleton is lying there, with a tiny skeleton stuck to its chest.

Father says:

'What's that? That thing on her?'

We say:

'It's a baby. Our little sister.'

Grandmother says:

'I did tell you to leave the dead in peace. Come and wash your hands in the kitchen.'

Father doesn't answer. He stares at the skeletons. His face is covered with sweat, tears and rain. He clambers with some difficulty out of the hole and walks off without turning round, his hands and clothes all muddy.

We ask Grandmother:

'What shall we do?'

She says:

'Fill in the hole again. What else can we do?'

We say:

'You go back into the warm, Grandmother. We'll see to all this.'

She goes back in.

We carry the skeletons in a blanket up into the attic, where we spread the bones out on straw to dry. Then we go back and fill in the hole in which nobody is lying any more.

Later, for months, we smooth and polish Mother's skull and bones and those of the baby, then we carefully reconstitute the skeleton by attaching each bone to thin pieces of wire. When we have finished our work, we hang Mother's skeleton from one of the attic beams and hang the baby's skeleton around her neck.

Our Father Comes Back

We don't see our father until several years later.

In the meantime, Grandmother had a new attack and we helped her to die as she had asked us to do. She is now buried in the same grave as Grandfather. Before they opened the grave, we recovered the treasure and hid it under the seat in front of our window, where the rifle, the cartridges and the grenades still are.

Father arrives one evening and asks:

'Where's your grandmother?'

'She's dead.'

'You live alone? How do you manage?'

'Very well, Father.'

He says:

'I've come here in hiding. You must help me.'

We say:

'You haven't given us any news of yourself for years.'

He shows us his hands. He no longer has any fingernails. They have been pulled out at the roots:

'I've just come out of prison. They tortured me.'

'Why?'

'I don't know. For no particular reason. I'm a politically suspect person. I'm not allowed to practise my profession. I'm under constant surveillance. My apartment is searched regularly. It's impossible for me to live much longer in this country.'

We say:

'You want to cross the frontier.'

He says:

'Yes. You live here, you must know . . .'

'Yes, we know. The frontier is uncrossable.'

Father lowers his head, looks at his hands for a moment, then says:

'There must be a weak spot somewhere. There must be some way of getting through.'

'At the risk of your life, yes.'

'I'd prefer to die rather than stay here.'

'You must make up your own mind, when you know the facts, Father.'

He says:

'I'm listening.'

We explain:

'The first problem is to get as far as the first barbed wire without meeting a patrol or being seen from one of the watchtowers. It can be done. We know the times of the patrols, and the positions of the watchtowers. The barbed-wire fence is one and a half metres high and one metre across. You need two planks of wood. One to climb on to the fence, the other to put on top of the fence so that you can stand up on it. If you lose your balance, you fall between the wires and you can't get out.'

Father says:

'I shan't lose my balance.'

We go on:

'You then have to get hold of the two planks of wood in order to get over the next fence in the same way, seven metres further on.'

Father laughs:

'It's child's play.'

'Yes, but the space between the two barriers is mined.'

Father goes pale:

'Then it's impossible.'

'No. It's a matter of luck. The mines are arranged in zig-zags, in Ws. If you walk in a straight line, you run the risk of walking on only one mine. If you take big steps, one has more or less a one in seven chance of avoiding it.'

Father thinks for a moment, then says:

'I'll risk it.'

We say:

'In that case, we are quite willing to help you. We'll go with you to the first fence.'

Father says:

'OK. Thanks. You wouldn't have something to eat, by any chance?'

We give him some bread and goat's cheese. We also offer him some wine from Grandmother's former vineyard. We pour into his glass a few drops of the sleeping draught that Grandmother was so good at making out of plants.

We take Father into our room and say:

'Good night. Sleep well. We'll wake you tomorrow.'

We go and sleep on the corner seat in the kitchen.

The Separation

Next morning, we get up very early. We make sure that Father is sleeping soundly.

We cut four planks of wood.

We dig up Grandmother's treasure: gold and silver coins and a lot of jewellery. We put most of it into a sack. We also take a grenade each, in case we are surprised by a patrol. If we eliminate the patrol, we can gain time.

We make a reconnaissance tour near the frontier in order to locate the best place: dead ground between two watchtowers. There, at the foot of a tall tree, we hide the sack and two of the planks.

We go back and eat. Later, we bring Father his breakfast. We have to shake him to wake him up. He rubs his eyes and says:

'I haven't slept so well for a long time.'

We place the tray on his knees. He says:

'What a feast! Milk, coffee, eggs, ham, butter, jam! These things are not to be found in the Big Town. How do you do it?'

'We work. Eat up, Father. We won't have time to give you another meal before you leave.'

He asks:

'I'll be going this evening?'

We say:

'You're going straight away. As soon as you're ready.'

He says:

'Are you crazy? I refuse to cross that bitch of a frontier

in broad daylight! We'll be seen!'

We say:

'We, too, have to see, Father. Only stupid people try to cross the frontier at night. At night there are four times as many patrols and the area is continually swept by search-lights. On the other hand, the surveillance is relaxed around eleven in the morning. The frontier guards think that nobody would be crazy enough to get through at that time.'

Father says:

'You're certainly right. I put myself in your hands.'

We ask:

'Will you allow us to search your pockets while you eat?'

'My pockets? Why?'

'You mustn't be identified. If anything happens to you and they learn that you are our father, we'll be accused of complicity.'

Father says:

'You think of everything.'

We say:

'We have to think of our own safety.'

We search his clothes. We take his papers, his identity card, his address book, a train ticket, bills and a photo-graph of Mother. We burn everything in the kitchen stove, except the photograph.

At eleven o'clock, we set off. Each of us carries a plank.

Father carries nothing. We ask him just to follow us and to make as little noise as possible. We get near the frontier. We tell Father to lie down behind the big tree and not to move.

Soon, a few metres away from us, a two-man patrol passes by. We can hear them talk:

'I wonder what there'll be to eat?'

'The same shit as usual, I expect.'

'There's shit and shit. Yesterday it was disgusting, but it's good sometimes.'

'Good? You wouldn't say that if you'd ever tasted my mother's soup.'

'I've never tasted your mother's soup. I've never had a mother. I've never eaten anything but shit. In the army, at least, I eat well occasionally.'

The patrol moves off. We say:

'Go on, Father. We have twenty minutes before the next patrol arrives.'

Father puts the two planks under his arm and moves forward. He places one of the planks against the fence and climbs up.

We lie face downwards behind the big tree, with our hands over our ears and our mouths open.

There is an explosion.

We run to the barbed wire with the other two planks and the sack.

Father is lying near the second fence.

Yes, there is a way of crossing the frontier: it's to get someone else to go first.

Picking up the sack, walking in Father's footsteps, then over his inert body, one of us goes into the other country.

The other one goes back to Grandmother's house.

SLAVOJ ŽIŽEK *Afterword*

There is a book through which I discovered what kind
of a person I really want to be: *The Notebook*, the first
volume of Agota Kristof's trilogy, which was followed by
The Proof and *The Third Lie*. When I first heard someone
talk about Agota Kristof, I thought it was an east Euro-
pean mispronunciation of Agatha Christie; but I soon discovered not only that Agota is not Agatha, but that Agota's
horror is much more terrifying than Agatha's.

The Notebook tells the story of young twins living with
their grandmother in a small Hungarian town during the
last years of the Second World War and the early years
of communism. The twins are thoroughly immoral – they
lie, blackmail, kill – yet they stand for authentic ethical
naivety at its purest. A couple of examples should suffice.
One day they meet a starving deserter in a forest and bring
him some things he asks them for.

> When we come back with the food and blanket, he says:
> 'You're very kind.'
> We say:
> 'We didn't want to be kind. We have brought you the
> things because you absolutely need them. That's all.'

If there ever was a Christian ethical stance, this is it: no
matter how weird their neighbour's demands, the twins
naively try to meet them. One night, they find themselves
sleeping in the same bed as a German officer, a tormented

gay masochist. Early in the morning, they awaken and want to leave the bed, but the officer holds them back:

> 'Don't move. Go back to sleep.'
> 'We want to urinate. We must go.'
> 'Don't go. Do it here.'
> We ask:
> 'Where?'
> He says:
> 'On me. Yes. Don't be afraid. Piss! On my face.'
> We do it, then we go out into the garden, because the bed is all wet.

A true work of love, if there ever was one! The twins' closest friend is a priest's housekeeper, a young voluptuous woman who washes them, playing erotic games with them. Then something happens when a procession of starved Jews is led through the town on their way to the camp:

> Just in front of us, a thin arm emerges from the crowd. A dirty hand is held out and a voice asks:
> 'Bread?'
> The housekeeper smiles and pretends to offer the rest of her bread; she holds it closer to the outstretched hand, then, with a great laugh, brings the piece of bread back to her mouth, takes a bite and says:
> 'I'm hungry, too.'

The boys decide to punish her: they put some ammunition into her kitchen stove so that when she lights it in the morning, it explodes and disfigures her. Along these lines, it is easy for me to imagine a situation in which I would be ready, without any moral qualms, to murder someone, even if I knew that this person did not kill anyone directly.

Reading reports about torture in Latin American military regimes, I found particularly repulsive the (regular) figure of a doctor who helped the actual torturers conduct their business in the most efficient way: he examined the victim and monitored the process, letting the torturers know how much the victim will be able to endure, what kind of tortures would inflict the most unbearable pain, etc. I must admit that if I were to encounter such a person, knowing that there is little chance of bringing him to legal justice, and be given the opportunity to murder him discreetly, I would simply do it, with a minimum of remorse about taking justice in my own hands.

What is crucial in such cases is to avoid the fascination of evil that propels us to elevate torturers into demonic transgressors who have the strength to overcome our petty moral considerations and act freely. Torturers are not beyond good and evil, they are beneath it. They do not heroically transgress our shared ethical rules, they simply lack them.

The two brothers also blackmail the priest: they threaten to let everybody know how he sexually molested Harelip, a girl who needs help to survive, demanding a weekly sum of money from him. The shocked priest asks them:

> 'It's monstrous. Have you any idea what you are doing?'
> 'Yes, sir. Blackmail.'
> 'At your age . . . It's deplorable.'
> 'Yes, it's deplorable that we've been forced to this. But Harelip and her mother absolutely need money.'

There is nothing personal in this blackmail: later, they even become close friends with the priest. When Harelip and her mother are able to survive on their own, they refuse further cash from the priest:

'Keep it. You have given enough. We took your money when it was absolutely necessary. Now we earn enough money to give some to Harelip. We've also taught her to work.'

Their cold-serving of others extends to killing them if asked: when their grandmother asks them to put poison into her cup of milk, they say:

'Don't cry, Grandmother. We'll do it; if you really want us to, we'll do it.'

Naive as it is, such a subjective attitude in no way precludes a monstrously cold reflexive distance. One day, the twins put on torn clothes and go begging. Passing women give them apples and biscuits and one of them even strokes their hair. Another woman invites them to her home to do some work, for which she will feed them.

We answer:
'We don't want to work for you, madam. We don't want to eat your soup or bread. We aren't hungry.'
She asks:
'Why are you begging, then?'
'To find out what effect it has and to observe people's reactions.'
She walks on, shouting:
'Dirty little hooligans! And cheeky with it!'
On our way home, we throw away the apples, biscuits and coins in the tall grass at the roadside.
It is impossible to throw away the stroking on our hair.

This is where I stand, how I would love to be: an ethical monster without empathy, doing what is to be done in a weird coincidence of blind spontaneity and reflexive distance, helping others while avoiding their disgusting proximity. With more people like this, the world would have been a pleasant place in which sentimentality would be replaced by a cold and cruel passion.

Ⓑ *editions*

Founded in 2007, CB editions publishes chiefly
short fiction (including work by Will Eaves, Gabriel
Josipovici, David Markson and May-Lan Tan)
and poetry (Andrew Elliott, Beverley Bie Brahic,
Nancy Gaffield, J. O. Morgan, D. Nurkse). Writers
published in translation include Apollinaire,
Andrzej Bursa, Joaquín Giannuzzi, Gert Hofmann,
Agota Kristof and Francis Ponge.

Books can be ordered from www.cbeditions.com.